THE VERY SOUND OF HIS HUSKY VOICE TRIGGERED A HOST OF NEVER FORGOTTEN RESPONSES. . . .

Unable to move, she was barely aware of the shallow rapidity of her breathing as Lance's cool gray-green gaze pinned her to the spot, studying every centimeter of her face, rediscovering in detail what his own lips had once possessed so completely.

With feather lightness his thumb slid across the velvet softness of her lips. Haley drew in a sharp breath, her heart thumping erratically as the rest of her body reacted wildly to the intimacy of Lance's touch. *This is ridiculous!* some inner voice screamed in objection. And yet, another part of her knew it was as it should be—as if their lips had already joined together in fiery reunion. . . .

A CANDLELIGHT ECSTASY ROMANCE ®

LOVE'S UNVEILING

Samantha Scott

A CANDLELIGHT ECSTASY ROMANCE ®

Published by
Dell Publishing Co., Inc.
1 Dag Hammarskjold Plaza
New York, New York 10017

ISBN: 0–440–15022–1

Printed in the United States of America
First printing—June 1983

With special thanks to Jacqueline Hamilton

To Our Readers:

We have been delighted with your enthusiastic response to Candlelight Ecstasy Romances®, and we thank you for the interest you have shown in this exciting series.

In the upcoming months we will continue to present the distinctive sensuous love stories you have come to expect only from Ecstasy. We look forward to bringing you many more books from your favorite authors and also the very finest work from new authors of contemporary romantic fiction.

As always, we are striving to present the unique, absorbing love stories that you enjoy most—books that are more than ordinary romance.

Your suggestions and comments are always welcome. Please write to us at the address below.

Sincerely,

The Editors
Candlelight Romances
1 Dag Hammarskjold Plaza
New York, New York 10017

CHAPTER ONE

Haley glanced around the green-tiled corridor in nervous anticipation. The medicinal smells inherent to a hospital created, as always, a knot of anxiety in the pit of her stomach. She brought her wrist up and checked her watch, surprised that only a minute had elapsed since the nurse had left her standing out here before going into Julia's room.

Strange, Haley thought, staring absently at the colorful flower arrangement in her hand. She'd have assumed this hospital visit would be taking place in the maternity ward—and under far happier circumstances. The last thing she'd have imagined Julia ever succumbing to was a nervous breakdown. Not the fun-loving, positive-minded girl she had supposedly known so well for all the years they'd been such close friends.

Haley shook her head of shoulder-length light auburn tresses, an unconscious effort to dispel the gloominess pressing in on her. So much had happened in the month she'd been back in Littleton. She hadn't even had time to assess the turn of events in her own life before being assaulted with the dramatic ones going on in her hometown.

The door to Julia's room opened just then, and a young nurse stepped soundlessly into the corridor carrying a tray with a disposable syringe that had been broken in half and an empty medicine vial.

"You can go in now," the nurse said quietly.

"Mrs. Sullivan has just received a sedative, though, so she might not be too alert the entire time."

Haley nodded her understanding. "Thank you. I won't stay too long."

"Are you a relative?"

"No. Julia and I have known each other for a long time though."

"Then stay as long as you like." The nurse smiled and cocked her head a bit to one side. "She needs friends now more than ever."

Haley managed a returning smile and pushed open the door. Julia's head was turned toward the window. Her slight form was obvious even from beneath the covers, evidence that she had lost a great deal of weight. A lump arose in Haley's throat, but she forced it back down as she closed the door and walked into the room.

"Julia?" she called out softly.

Slowly Julia's head turned, her features offering Haley only a blank, lifeless stare that was barely recognizable as belonging to that of her longtime friend. Once-sparkling green eyes were now vacant and lackluster, so pronounced a difference from the way Haley remembered them that the effect was truly shocking.

"Hello, Haley." Julia spoke finally, the flatness of her tone matching the dullness of her expression.

"Julia. . . . I'm sorry I haven't gotten in touch with you until now," Haley began awkwardly, taking a few steps into the room. "I thought it would be better if I—"

"It doesn't matter," Julia interrupted quietly. She accepted the flowers Haley handed her but merely stared at them as though not quite sure what to do with them.

"Here," Haley offered, "I'll put them somewhere for you." She glanced around the room. "You have so many, I don't know if there's any room." She hesitated, then smiled brightly. "Maybe I can make room between these on the dresser."

Julia made no move to hand the vase to her, so Haley gently took it from her and placed it on the dresser between several others.

She sat down in a straight-backed chair next to the bed, feeling distinctly uncomfortable and not knowing what she should or shouldn't say. But suddenly Julia solved her dilemma, her voice suddenly coming to life. Her eyes, however, shone curiously with an odd, piercing glint. Haley felt the skin at the back of her neck prickle in response.

"I knew he would do this." The words hissed from between Julia's pouting lips. "I knew he would leave me. But"—she stared straight ahead, her voice dropping to hardly more than a whisper—"I never thought it would be this way in the beginning. I thought I could make him happy, make him love me." Her dull green eyes began swirling with riotous emotions, and Haley shifted uncomfortably in her seat. Julia's behavior was so strange, so totally unexpected, it was almost frightening in its intensity.

"But all he ever cared about was his stupid restaurant business," Julia burst forth angrily. "Do you know how many he's opened since we were married? Fifteen! Can you imagine how much time he's had left for me?" Her eyes widened as she spat out bitterly, "None! None at all!"

13

"Julia, I didn't—"

"Oh, I know you'd rather not hear about this," Julia interrupted, her mood swinging to one of self-pity, her previously animated face sagging dejectedly.

"No, it's not that at all," Haley objected. "I do want to listen to you, Julia. I want us to talk like old times."

Julia didn't appear to be listening now, though, and she slipped down in her bed, tucking the covers up under her chin and turning her head to stare out the window as before.

"I don't know what made me ever think he would love me," she whispered in a ghostly tone. "I don't even know why Lance ever married me. He just never loved me, I know that now." Julia turned then to face Haley once more, her eyes rounding as she said sweetly, "You know, I've often thought he'd have been happier with someone like you, Haley. Someone strong and sure of herself. Not someone weak and stupid like me."

"Oh, Julia, how can you say that?" Haley stood and approached the bed, placing a hand on her friend's shoulder. "You were always a strong person. I was the one who always relied on your advice, remember?" She attempted a smile. "I was always too busy with my nose in a book."

Julia's long lashes blinked once, as if she remembered those days when the two of them had been inseparable. But the memory was a fleeting one, immediately replaced with an expression of sadness and withdrawal. "That was a long time ago," she mur-

mured. "I'm sick now, they tell me. Why else would I be here?"

"But you're going to be all right," Haley said encouragingly. "Nothing's wrong with getting help when things get rough. Just give it time."

God, I sound so trite, Haley thought. But what else could she offer? It was totally unrealistic to pretend that after a two-and-a-half year absence she could step right back into the relationship they had once shared, as if nothing had changed. But then everything had changed, even before Haley had left Littleton—at least for Haley it had. And all of it, she admitted painfully, was her own fault. Hers and Lance's.

It was incredible how the mere mention of Lance's name set off a powerful emotional response she had believed was completely behind her. Haley swallowed deeply, unable to force back the shame, the guilt roiling within. Suddenly she was seized with an intense desire to escape this gloomy hospital room, this friend who seemed so like a stranger now.

Julia spoke out suddenly, and Haley jerked reflexively. "Lance doesn't care how sick I am!"

"Of course, he does," Haley reassured her, wishing for all the world the nurse—anyone!—would walk in and tell her to leave.

"Ha!" Julia emitted a gruff laugh. "He doesn't give a damn about what's happened to me." Her tone dripped venom and her once lovely face contorted in a nasty sneer. "I wish something would happen to his damn restaurant chain. Then *he'd* find out what it's like to lose something you love."

"Julia," Haley said slowly, trying desparately to

control the waver in her voice, "you shouldn't say that. I'm sure Lance would have—" She stopped abruptly, her words falling on deaf ears as Julia turned her head, her rage apparently spent for the moment. Haley stared at her, not sure whether to go on. After a while Julia's eyelids began to flutter then fell heavily over her eyes. Haley supposed she was responding to the sedative the nurse had given her earlier. She watched for a few minutes as Julia's chest began to rise and fall rhythmically as she drifted off to sleep.

Soundlessly Haley picked up her purse from the chair and turned and walked out of the room, grateful to be closing the door behind her.

Stopping just outside the door in the corridor, Haley drew in a deep breath, willing herself to a more composed state. Acceptance of everything she'd just observed would come later, she told herself; for the moment she just needed to get ahold of her emotions.

She walked slowly back toward the nurses' station, slipping her arms into the fawn suede blazer she had taken off earlier. Not until she was almost at the circular desk that served as the nurses' station did she look straight ahead, her amber eyes gazing in disbelieving shock at the looming figure standing with his back toward her.

Haley stopped dead in her tracks; a part of her wanting to run and hide, another more forceful part rooting her to the spot.

It had been two and a half years since she'd last seen Lance Sullivan, two and a half years in which she'd tried to force the memory of him and what had transpired between them from her mind.

But this one breathtaking moment was all it took to reveal with crystal clarity that it had all been time wasted. The mere sight of Lance standing there, speaking quietly with one of the nurses, shook her to the very core, transporting her back through all those wasted months of trying to make him into nothing more than a memory.

Time was condensed into barely perceptible moments; it seemed like yesterday that the two of them had shared each other so completely, so consumingly. And suddenly the hopeless anguish of what they had done came flooding back full force, renewing the terrible guilt she believed had been paid for.

Haley heard Lance speaking to the nurse, then watched him fold the sheaf of papers he'd been holding and slip them in the inner pocket of his overcoat. He turned, took one step, and then stopped abruptly, staring at her as if she were a ghost. Some nameless emotion swept across the hard, angular planes of his face, disappearing rapidly as he moved toward her in long, easy strides.

Haley willed herself to camouflage the emotions threatening to play havoc with her already delicate composure, but it was an almost overwhelming effort. As he walked toward her, her heart began pounding at the mere sight of him: the same virile, impenetrable Lance Sullivan—as tawny and self-assured as ever. His hair was still a little too long, falling in a disarray of golden brown curls beneath his ears and on his nape. He stopped a few feet away from her, standing with feet slightly apart, one fisted hand just below his waist.

"Hello, Lance," Haley greeted him, surprised at

17

the evenness of her tone. Her fingernails were digging into the leather material of her clutch bag.

"I heard you were back in town," Lance said, his lids narrowing over smoky green eyes as they slowly, almost languorously surveyed her appearance from head to toe. "You've become even more beautiful."

Haley could feel her skin warming as she responded to the intimacy of his visual caress, and she swallowed spasmodically. Her mouth felt incredibly dry, yet she managed to answer him coolly. "I just left Julia's room. She's asleep."

Lance nodded once and cocked an eyebrow. "She does a lot of that lately," he commented dryly.

Haley frowned. "You certainly don't sound very sympathetic, Lance. She's very sick, in case you didn't know."

"Is that so?" Obviously he couldn't have cared less about his ex-wife's condition. Haley wondered what he was doing here. For that matter her own presence was in question.

She glanced at her watch and took a step forward. "Tell her good-bye for me, will you? I need to get back to work now. If you'll ex—"

"Just a minute," Lance interrupted, reaching out and placing a hand on her forearm.

Haley's gaze riveted on the hair-darkened hand resting on her arm, then slanted upward to meet the gray-green eyes studying her so intently.

"I want to talk to you," Lance said, removing his hand. "I'd come to deliver these insurance papers to Julia, but since she's asleep, I can leave them with the nurse."

"Lance, I—" Haley hesitated, her gaze shifting

18

beneath the intensity of his. "I really am in a hurry." She glanced up at him again. "And there is nothing we have to talk about."

"Why don't you let me be the judge of that, since it was my suggestion," Lance inserted dryly. "Surely you have time for a cup of coffee. We can visit the coffee shop downstairs."

Haley's breath shuddered as she drew it in then expelled it. "I'm sorry, Lance. I really do have to get back to work."

"That's all I'm asking. To talk to you about your work."

Haley frowned. "What do you mean?"

"I'll tell you about it downstairs," he said firmly, cupping her elbow in his hand, propelling her alongside him as he walked down the corridor toward the elevators.

For an afternoon chat the hospital coffee shop was certainly lacking in charm and atmosphere, but Haley couldn't have been more grateful for the clinical surroundings. The noise and crowd created a distraction she sorely needed. Being so near the man she had spent two and a half years doing everything in her power to forget was more than she could have handled under any less austere circumstances.

After paying for their cups of coffee, Lance led the way toward one of the few unoccupied tables. He pulled out a chair for Haley, and she sat down, too jittery to add to the problem by drinking the stimulating liquid. Nevertheless, she sipped at it absently, anxious and curious as to what Lance was leading up to.

"How long have you been back in Littleton?" he

19

inquired, propping both elbows on the table after stirring his coffee.

"A month," Haley replied curtly. "Lance, I—"

"Why don't you just relax for a minute or two," Lance interrupted, a corner of his mouth lifting in a wry grin. "Surely you didn't imagine we'd never run into each other. Although I must say, you've kept yourself under cover very well since you've been back," he added.

Despite his suggestion Haley was far from being able to relax. "I've had quite a lot to do," she answered. "Setting oneself up in business is not the easiest thing in the world, you know."

Lance brought his cup to his lips and sipped, then set it back down on the table and nodded. "Yes. I'd heard that's what you were up to. Very commendable, I must say. I always did admire your artistic talent—among other things."

Haley's face and neck flushed hotly. "I don't need this, Lance Sullivan," she spat out angrily, her hand accidentally colliding with her cup of coffee, spilling some of it onto the table. "Dammit!" She shoved her chair back quickly, trying to avoid the coffee dripping off the edge of the table. Lance grabbed several paper napkins from the dispenser and began blotting up the spill.

"Just stay where you are," he ordered, and Haley chafed inwardly as she found herself doing just that.

"What do you want from me?" she demanded harshly. "Surely you don't expect me to sit here and listen to your insults."

"I wasn't insulting you." Lance spoke calmly, convincingly. Haley's amber gaze softened slightly, and some of the rigidness left her shoulders.

Lance studied her for a long, thoughtful moment, then said, "I want you to take on a job for me. As an art consultant. That is your business, isn't it?"

Haley's eyes narrowed warily. "Yes, it is. But how did you know?"

Lance dismissed the question with a shrug. "Very little in this town escapes my attention." His gaze was hard, uncompromising.

"What is it you really want, Lance?" Haley asked.

"I told you. I want you to work for me. On one of my pet projects."

Haley tilted her head to one side and lifted an eyebrow questioningly. "Oh? Which one is that?"

"I'm opening a restaurant in Canada," Lance explained, his gray-green eyes sparkling with an unmistakable glimmer of enthusiasm. "My first outside the United States. It will have the same Sullivan style, naturally, but with a Canadian flavor. It was almost more trouble than it was worth, plowing through all the red tape necessary to obtain a permit to even build the damn thing, but," he added, gesturing with one hand, "it's nearing completion at last."

"But why do you need me?" Haley asked. "Why don't you just hire the same people you've used all along for your other restaurants?"

"Because," Lance explained patiently, "as I said, this one is special. I know your talent, and I believe you're the most qualified person for the job."

Such a pat answer had to have a catch somewhere, Haley thought suspiciously. Especially coming from

Lance Sullivan. "My field is art consulting, not interior decorating," Haley stated carefully.

"Yes, I'm aware of that. I want artwork to be the primary focus of this restaurant. It should provide an atmosphere that is conducive to a more educated, cultivated clientele."

Haley tapped a fingernail on the table, her expression pensive. "Where in Canada is the restaurant located?"

"It's in Banff. A small tourist village sixty or so miles west of Calgary in Alberta. Western Canada."

"Right. I know about it," Haley said, skepticism temporarily overshadowed by genuine curiosity. "My sister was there for a week of skiing a couple of years ago. Quite a beautiful locale you've chosen."

"Well"—Lance smiled broadly, spreading one hand before him, palm outward—"are you interested in the position?"

Haley regarded him warily, every instinct alerted to the persuasive charm she had fallen victim to once before. "I suppose I should admit that I'm flattered by the offer," she answered finally, idly circling a thumb around the rim of her cup. "It's not that I couldn't use the work. It—I just . . ." Her voice trailed off.

"You just what?" Lance prompted.

Haley's expression was reproachful as she retorted sharply, "All right, Lance. Let's just stop the games, shall we? You know damn well what's going on in my head right now." She laughed gruffly. "I guess Julia had a point. You really *don't* give a damn about anything but your restaurant chain! For God's sake, Lance. . . . Your ex-wife is lying upstairs in a hospital

22

bed, and all you can talk about is your next conquest!" Haley's brow tightened, and her throat constricted painfully as she asked, "What did happen between the two of you?"

Lance's eyes focused on some distant point beyond her shoulder, and for a moment Haley was doubtful she would get an answer to her question. She watched as an angry storm brewed behind his carefully controlled features, and the muscles along the angular line of his jaw twitched revealingly. Slowly his eyelids narrowed, and he shifted his gaze to stare intently at her.

"What happened?" he muttered, bitterness deepening the grooves on either side of his mouth. "*You* can ask that, knowing everything you do? Marrying Julia was a mistake from the beginning, just as I said it would be. Are you still so blind that you can't understand that something like this was bound to happen?" His gaze shifted away from hers, then swung back abruptly. "No, I don't suppose you can," he added disdainfully. "You were just as much a child as she was."

What a consummate actor the man was, Haley thought furiously, and she'd be damned if she was going to sit here and listen to this garbage. Hadn't two and a half years wrought any change in him at all? She'd made a mistake accepting Lance's invitation to have coffee. She should have left before giving in to the darker, more emotional side of her nature—the side that had never really forgotten the man, never successfully erased what she had once felt for him.

Suddenly she could no longer sit here willingly,

discussing a subject that was still painful to everyone concerned, especially the poor woman lying upstairs tearing her heart out over a man who had been only toying with her love for him. A man who had found it all to easy to seduce her best friend.

Haley's chair scraped noisily as she pushed it back across the linoleum floor. She reached for her clutch bag and sat posed on the edge of her seat as she spoke. "Lance, I think it best that I leave. I don't see any point in continuing this discussion. We've said all that can be said about the matter, and it'll do no good to hash it all over again."

"Still the little coward, aren't you?" Lance inserted bitingly, his gaze burning, penetrating now. "Still afraid of your feelings. Afraid to admit that you're a woman with needs, a—"

"Lance, please," Haley interrupted, rising from the chair, emotion balling up like a tight fist in the center of her stomach. "I have to go." She started to take a step away, then stopped, adding in a tremulous voice, "And I'm truly sorry about Julia. I'll do anything I can to help her." She paused, then added accusingly, "We were best friends, after all."

"As if I could forget that," Lance threw back caustically, lifting his cup and throwing down the rest of his now cold coffee. He pushed back his chair and stood, but made no move to follow her.

"Nice seeing you again, Haley," he said, the tightness of his features relaxing as he cast her a heart-stopping grin. "If you change your mind about the offer, don't hesitate to give me a call."

"Good-bye, Lance," Haley said shakily. Swallowing spasmodically, she turned on her heel, willing her feet to walk at a normal pace, her heart totally un-cooperative as it pounded in her chest at a frighten-ing rate.

Not nearly as frightening, though, as the traitor-ous response of the rest of her body, falling victim, as always, to the mere presence of Lance Sullivan.

CHAPTER TWO

Haley pulled into her private parking space and walked across the tree-lined drive to her town house, oblivious to the breathtaking backdrop of the distant Colorado Rockies. Letting herself inside the fenced patio, she fumbled inside her purse for a moment, finally extracting her key and inserting it into the lock of the front door. Her actions were performed mechanically; her mind was preoccupied with the unexpected turn of events the day had provided. The sound of the telephone did not pierce her consciousness until the fourth ring, and she shut the door behind her, hurrying toward the inconspicuous Princess model on the bar that separated the kitchen from the dining area.

"Hello?" she answered, slightly breathless. She kicked off her shoes and sat down in one of two cane-backed barstools.

"Hi, honey," her mother's voice greeted her. "Did you just get in? I called several times this afternoon, and you didn't answer."

"As a matter of fact, I just walked in the door. Just a second, Mom." Placing the receiver on the countertop, she slipped out of her jacket then reached up and removed her pierced earrings. Picking up the telephone, she carried it as far as the cord would stretch, plopping down in her favorite wingback chair.

"Okay. I'm back."

"You sound really tired," her mother commented. "Doesn't sound as though you'll be too receptive to my invitation."

"Oh? What's that?"

"Nothing much really. I just thought you might like to join your father and me for supper. The weather's rather nice, so I thought we might grill some steaks on the patio."

"Oh. . . . Gosh, Mom, any other time and I'd take you up on it," Haley replied. "But all I want to do tonight is take a hot bath and crawl into bed with a book. I'm not even hungry."

"Haley," her mother began in a tone Haley recognized immediately, "I realize how important it is to you to get your business off the ground, but as I've told you before, there's certainly no rush. Your father and I are perfectly willing to help you out with anything you need."

"I know, Mom," Haley replied patiently. "And believe me, I'd take you up on the offer if I needed to. But I'm doing fine financially." She hesitated, then sighed, explaining, "I just got back from the hospital. Seeing Julia wasn't exactly an uplifting experience."

"Why, honey? What happened?" Mrs. Jordenson was genuinely surprised. "Mrs. Morris told me she was coming along just fine."

"Well, I don't know. Maybe she's just putting on an act for her parents. She's certainly nothing like the Julia Morris I used to know."

"I'm really sorry to hear that." Mrs. Jordenson sounded truly saddened by the news. "You know, it just seems impossible that such a beautiful, vivacious

27

girl could end up like she has. Of course, I always did think she was a little flighty at times, but I certainly never would have thought she'd suffer a nervous breakdown. Do you suppose it was the divorce, honey?"

"Oh, I'm sure it was," Haley answered, bitterness edging her tone. "That's practically all she talked about while I was there. How Lance ignored her during their marriage, how he invested all his time and interest in his restaurant business."

Mrs. Jordenson clucked her tongue. "Well, I can't figure it out. I thought they made such a darling pair. And Julia seemed so devoted to him."

"Mmm." Haley put a hand on her forehead, pressing fingertips against the dull throbbing that had started in one temple.

"You really do sound exhausted, dear," Mrs. Jordenson commented. "I'll let you go, but your father and I *would* like to have you over Friday night for supper."

"That sounds great, Mom," Haley said. "I'll give you a call before then. And, Mom?"

"Yes?"

"Is Dad doing all right?"

"He's fine, dear. Don't you worry about him. Just be sure and get plenty of rest, and we'll see you on Friday."

"Okay. Good night, Mom."

"Good night, honey."

Haley put the receiver back in its cradle and stared at it for a moment before standing and placing the telephone on the bar.

What a day, she reflected, picking up her purse

and shoes and climbing the stairs to her bedroom. It was her favorite room in the town house. Muted gray walls blended peacefully with a pale peach flower-patterned bedspread; the same delicate shade was repeated throughout the room. Taking off her clothes and hanging them in the spacious walk-in closet, she slipped into a warm, navy-blue terry-cloth robe and walked into the bathroom to turn on the taps in the tub.

Bending forward, she swooped up her light auburn tresses into a topknot and applied cream to her face, leaving it on to be rinsed off in the bath.

Looking at her white, creamed face in the mirror, Haley was faintly amused at the apparition she made. Out of the blue, she found herself wondering what Lance would think if he could see her looking like this, completely the opposite of the picture of sophistication she'd made earlier today. Instantly she chastised herself for the ridiculous notion. The last thing she needed on her mind now was Lance Sullivan.

Ridding herself of the robe, Haley climbed slowly into the water, relishing the rush of pleasure as the steaming water made contact with the cooler temperature of her skin.

Resting against the sloping back of the tub, Haley closed her eyes, willing her mind blank, a condition with which her brain refused to cooperate: Lance Sullivan was still very much on her mind. Ruefully she admitted she wasn't going to have an easy time of stopping further thoughts about him either, especially considering the interesting offer he'd made for her to work on his newest restaurant. It was, she thought sadly, the only offer she'd had to date.

Of course, she'd only officially been in business a little over ten days, so she really hadn't expected to have that much going right now. What could help more than anything was a project exactly like this one, one that would undoubtedly look quite impressive in her portfolio.

Slipping down to immerse herself up to her chin in the deliciously refreshing water, Haley sighed slowly, unable to stave off what was really on her mind.

Reluctantly she admitted she couldn't fool herself a moment longer. As much as she wanted to deny it, she'd fallen victim once more—swiftly and dangerously—to that same magnetism that had pulled her and Lance Sullivan together in the beginning. She could feel it working on her very soul, chipping away the delicate wall of defense she had so painstakingly erected.

An unexpected shiver coursed its way down her spine as memories flooded her mind, memories of those terribly guilt-ridden events of two and a half years ago, events that had necessitated her leaving Littleton as soon as possible after Lance and Julia's wedding.

She had known there was absolutely no way she could remain in the same small community with the two of them living as husband and wife. She had needed desperately to get away, to try and begin a completely different life of her own.

God knows she had certainly never intended for things to go as far as they had. Yet, she wondered how it would have even been possible had Julia not insisted on throwing them together in the first place. The consequences of the supposedly "friendly" relationship between the three of them had exceeded anything Haley could have initially imagined.

Haley and Julia had been constant companions ever since they were ten years old—sharing school years, vacations, experiences with boyfriends, even attending the University of Colorado together, although their ambitions had been vastly different.

Haley fully intended to acquire a degree that would provide her with a future in commercial art. She had no clear-cut ideas as to what direction that future would take, but she was headstrong in making the most of her education.

Julia, on the other hand, majored in Having Fun and Acquiring As Many Boyfriends As Possible; she took the easiest courses available, ones that would leave adequate time for her to indulge in everything necessary to provide her with both pursuits. Her eager, fun-loving personality was the perfect complement to her blond, green-eyed beauty, which never failed to attract a bevy of constant admirers, both male and female.

At times, however, there had been a peculiar intensity about her best friend that Haley had often puzzled over. It seemed as if Julia were always waiting for something more exciting than she had so far experienced—some issue or person to really sink her teeth into.

That someone came along in their senior year at the university, at one of the many parties Julia attended more faithfully than any of her classes. This

31

one happened to be a birthday party for a friend of hers held at Sullivan's, one of Denver's more renowned supper clubs.

Haley, having had other plans for the evening, naturally received a full report of the festivities, but Julia's carrying on about the fantastic man she'd met exceeded anything Haley had ever observed of her friend. Within a month of dating Lance Sullivan—heir to the vast chain of Sullivan restaurants located now in practically every major city in the United States—Julia was hopelessly in love.

Haley was suspicious from the beginning that Julia was perhaps more impressed with Lance than he was with her. It seemed to Haley that most of the plans the two of them made had been initiated by Julia; Haley was afraid—in spite of the changing times, which encouraged women to be more aggressive in pursuing relationships—that Julia was perhaps making the mistake of chasing Lance.

Nevertheless, the relationship appeared to be working, and by Christmas Julia had secured herself a beautiful diamond engagement ring. It was at their engagement party that Haley met Lance for the first time. Normally she met all of Julia's boyfriends either at school or at Julia's apartment, but Lance had rarely visited Julia at her place, at least not when Haley had been there.

One glance revealed to Haley that Julia had not been exaggerating when she described Lance. Haley found herself impressed not only with his looks but with his ample charm and obvious intelligence, qualities all too rarely found in the same man. After being introduced to him that evening, Haley had observed the couple quietly from the sidelines as the party progressed, spending most of her time in conversation with Julia's mother and father.

At one point during the evening Haley had the distinct feeling that she was being watched. She turned, her eyes riveting on the pair that had chosen to single her out. Haley would never forget the intense wave of shock that coursed through her as she felt the effect of Lance's piercing gaze. Strangely enough she wasn't surprised by his stare. With a sense of déjà vu she was aware that she had been expecting it—had even wanted it.

She had turned away quickly, of course, not wanting the awkward scene to be observed by anyone. She was seized with an inexplicable guilt, too, although absolutely nothing had occurred except that Julia's fiancé had simply stared at her for a little longer than was necessary or appropriate. Nevertheless, she could not deny some nameless overwhelming emotion, at once both frightening and strangely exciting.

Later she had puzzled over the brief incident, wondering if perhaps she had merely imagined that Lance Sullivan had appeared as drawn to her as she had been to him. But such a thing could happen anytime and anywhere, she had reasoned, and had shrugged it off as just one of those things that were best forgotten.

And she *had* been fairly successful at forgetting it for a while. Then in February Julia had invited her to a dinner party that she was giving at her apartment for Lance's birthday. Instinctively Haley had wanted to refuse, but Julia had insisted, saying she was absolutely dependent on her presence.

Haley had finally relented, deciding to invite Steve, an engineering student she had been dating frequently. As it turned out, the evening proved to be every bit as disturbing as she had feared it might.

Lance had said or done nothing to indicate any other feeling for her besides a certain polite friendliness. Haley began to wonder if she was merely imagining that there was something behind his proper demeanor, something that went deeper than surface interest.

Yet, as the night went on, he did seem to focus much of the conversation on Haley and her plans for a future in the commercial art field. He dealt with such specialists frequently in his line of business, he informed her, and she was drawn by his easy manner of conversing, completely taken by the man's sincere interest in her work and aspirations.

The night had ended on an entirely pleasant note, leaving Haley happy for Julia; happy that her friend had chosen such an amicable man to marry. She even convinced herself that the remoteness she'd observed in Lance's attitude toward Julia was only imagined on her part. Surely it was merely Lance's preference to abstain from exhibiting affection in public that made his interest in Julia seem superficial compared to Julia's in him. Oh, he liked her enough; that was obvious, Haley thought. But the idea continued to niggle at Haley: that that was the extent of his emotion toward her best friend.

But then, she'd reflected later, who was she to judge something she really knew very little about?

She didn't discover how accurate her observation

had been until a couple of weeks later, the week Julia left with her family to attend her grandmother's funeral in New York. Haley's reaction to Lance's request to see her had been one of both surprise and excitement tinged with more than a shadow of guilt. She hadn't refused, however, and Lance had offered no excuses for wanting to see her. Their meetings that week, and those the following, had been conducted in careful privacy, opening up to Haley a world of longing and passion she hadn't dreamed possible.

Reflecting back now, with the perspective of two and a half years, she wished she could have found the strength to call a halt to the wrongful affair that first week. It wasn't as if she hadn't tried. She had, in fact—several times. But, as always, Lance had been stronger and terribly persuasive, and the painful guilt-ridden affair had gone on even after Julia had returned.

Lance had insisted that he didn't love Julia, had made a mistake in becoming engaged to her, an idea he'd thought was acceptable in the beginning but now realized was completely wrong. He would have never got himself into such a situation, he claimed, had he known Haley previously.

Haley had wanted to believe Lance, having already become more emotionally involved with him than she was able to deal with. The thought of what their affair might do to Julia was much too devastating even to consider continuing it. Julia was head over heels in love with Lance and nothing could ever make Haley hurt her oldest and dearest friend.

Haley had insisted that her first loyalty lay with

Julia, but she'd had a most difficult time convincing Lance of the fact. Lance felt their attraction for each other precluded any other loyalties, both on his part and on hers, and had sworn that he could not live a lie, that he would tell Julia the truth and break off their engagement.

Like a diver taking a deep breath before a long fearful plunge, Haley had waited, finally willing to take whatever consequences would come from Lance's determined stance. She had been shocked beyond belief, therefore, when Julia announced shortly afterward that she and Lance were moving their wedding date from June to April—only a month away.

Haley had not spoken another word to Lance after the shattering news, disguising her anguish behind a painfully constructed facade of happiness for the both of them, even going so far as to help Julia with the last-minute details of the wedding. She was blindly determined to prove to Lance that she couldn't care less about what he had done: his lying, his taking her emotions for granted, his playing both sides of the fence in what was a cruel game, his not giving a damn whom he hurt in the process.

Julia hadn't even bothered to complete the semester that year. She declared that she had no need for a degree now, planning, as she told everyone, to devote herself to Lance and their marriage. A complete turnaround for the former playgirl, now a woman who was totally, incurably in love.

Haley was graduated from the university in late May; none too soon as far as she was concerned. She had known even before Julia's wedding that she couldn't stay here in Littleton, nor even in Denver, the nearby metropolis. It would be far too much of a burden to endure living in the same community where Julia was now establishing herself as Mrs. Lance Sullivan, social butterfly. Haley had to accept that the innocent friendship she and Julia had shared over the years had been irrevocably shattered; that their relationship would never be the same again.

Of course, Julia would never have to know any of what had happened between Haley and Lance. Haley had simply made it known that she wanted the experience of living somewhere other than in her hometown, reasoning that distance and time would create different worlds for all three of them, and would push the past further and further from their minds and hearts.

To a certain degree her theory had proved correct. Gone was any remnant of the strong feeling she'd once had about Julia's friendship, and now, of course, considering all that had happened to the poor woman, Haley found it particularly difficult to believe Julia was the same friend with whom she had shared her youth.

The theory had failed miserably, however, in her acceptance of what had occurred between her and Lance. Haley had never been able to erase the gnawing pain his cold-blooded deception had buried deep in her heart. Two years in Philadelphia had come and gone quickly. Though she had learned a great deal, none of the knowledge had been useful in settling the old hurts.

Today had brought them back upon her full force,

37

afflicting her with a weariness that claimed her mind as well as her body. And it was an aching weariness, one she could have lived without at this time in her life.

Had she known she would be smack-dab in the middle of the triangle she had left Littleton to escape, she could just as easily have settled in an apartment in or around Denver. Perhaps it wouldn't have been as convenient for her to see her parents as often as she was able to now, but since Haley's primary reason for moving back here had been to be near her father, who had developed a mild coronary problem, she would have been more than willing to make the effort.

"Ah, well," Haley whispered, "enough soul-searching and rehashing for one night." Willing herself to let go of it all, at least for a while, she reached for a bottle of bath gel and her Loofa sponge and began working up a vigorous, stimulating lather from head to toe.

The bath was effective, working better than any artificial sedative, and by the time Haley donned one of her long silk nightgowns, her eyes were drooping heavily. Enough for one day, she thought just before drifting off into a sound sleep. More than enough.

CHAPTER THREE

The rest of the week fairly flew by. Haley spent much of it in her car, threading her way among familiar streets and highways of Denver, making as many contacts as possible. It seemed as though she'd covered every sort of office building that Denver had to offer, from huge corporate high rises to small shopping centers. She hoped that her specialty, proposing and installing original or reproduced works of art for newly built and refurbished places of business, would include a large, varied clientele.

The feedback she was receiving was promising, but not particularly concrete, and by Friday evening her spirits were somewhat low at not having got anywhere.

Remembering she was to have dinner with her parents that night, Haley forced all thoughts of business aside, not wanting to give either of them, especially her father, cause for worry.

After a quick shower she dressed casually in a pair of gray wool slacks and a pale green pullover, then drove the short distance to her parents' home. It was a large contemporary house, the one in which Haley had spent her last three years of high school. The sounds and smells of home affected her immediately, setting to rest the tension and worry she had carried around all day.

"Haley, is that you?" her mother called out from the kitchen.

"Yeah," Haley yelled back. "Be there in a sec." She shrugged out of her coat and hung it in the hall closet. She ducked her head inside the den as she walked down the hallway toward the kitchen.

"Hi, Dad." She greeted her father with a smile. Ernest Jordenson was reclining in his favorite lounge chair in front of the television, and he turned to grin at his youngest daughter.

"Hello, baby," he greeted her cheerily. "Come on in and watch the news with me."

"I'd better help Mom in the kitchen first. See you in a minute."

"Okay." With a nod Mr. Jordenson turned his attention back to the news program.

Haley found her mother in the kitchen, the heels of her sling-back pumps clicking smartly on the Mexican-style tiled floor as she crossed from oven to sink and back again, seeing to the finishing touches for their supper before setting it on the dining-room table.

"Mmm, smells divine," Haley commented, helping herself to a sliver of deliciously seasoned meat from the warming platter. "Tastes fantastic too. As usual."

"You got here early," Rita Jordenson commented, popping a foil-wrapped loaf of French bread into the oven.

Haley glanced at her watch. "No, I didn't. You said seven o'clock, and it's five after now."

"I meant, earlier than I expected you." Mrs. Jordenson gave her daughter a critical appraisal. "Honey, you look exhausted. Have you been getting any rest at all?"

"Of course, I have, Mom," Haley answered, a trifle irritated by her mother's scrutiny. "I just happened to have an extraordinarily long—and unsuccessful—day."

Mrs. Jordenson said nothing, but she frowned as she began carrying dishes of food to the table in the adjacent dining room. "Haley, could you pour the tea while I get all this on the table?"

"Sure," Haley answered, setting about the task immediately, eager to change the subject. Her relief, however, was short-lived, she discovered as soon as the three of them sat down to eat.

After a few minutes of discussing Haley's older sister, Greta, who lived with her husband and two children in Tucson, Mr. Jordenson steered the conversation around to Haley's new venture in establishing herself as an art consultant.

Ernest Jordenson, an attractive man in his early sixties, pushed back his plate after his first serving, a gesture in keeping with his cardiologist's advice and his own good intentions. He leaned back in his chair, fingers absently toying with his napkin, an unconscious effort to distract himself from his normal habit of lighting up a cigarette.

"George told me you spoke to Lance the other day," he said, referring to his longtime business associate George Sullivan.

Haley glanced up in vague surprise. She certainly hadn't expected the conversation to take this particular turn.

"Yes . . . I did," she replied. "I was visiting Julia in the hospital, and I ran into Lance in the hallway as I was leaving." She shrugged, as if to express the unimportance of the meeting.

She started to change the subject, when surprisingly her father cut in—somewhat hastily at that. "And did the two of you get a chance to talk?" he asked.

Again Haley was puzzled by her father's interest. Certainly never a neglectful father, he had nevertheless always excluded himself from any of the gossip his wife and daughters indulged in. Haley glanced from her father to her mother. Her mother had suddenly become quietly absorbed in finishing up what little remained on her plate. Confused by her parents' uncharacteristic behavior, she turned back to her father.

"Yes. As a matter of fact, we had a cup of coffee together."

Mr. Jordenson reached for his glass of iced tea and took a sip, set it back down on the table, then pursed his lips together to blot off the excess liquid.

"Why do you ask?" Haley queried, laying her fork down and staring curiously at her father.

Her mother's chair brushed softly across the plush carpeting as she pushed it back. "I'll be right back. I want to take that pie out of the oven. I think it's warm enough."

Haley frowned as she watched her mother scurry out of the room.

"What's going on here?" Haley asked. "If you don't mind my saying so, you two are acting really weird."

Ernest Jordenson relaxed at his daughter's apt observation, his gray eyes sparkling with a mischievous, almost guilty glint.

"I suppose we are acting a bit unusual," he conceded with a brief chuckle. "But I just didn't know how to bring the subject up other than to ask you in a roundabout way what Lance Sullivan talked to you about."

Haley peered at her father, trying for the life of her to guess what he was leading up to.

Haley shrugged. "All right. I'll tell you. He asked me to do some work for him at one of the new restaurants he's opening in Canada. One of his pet projects, he claimed."

Mr. Jordenson's posture straightened a little at his daughter's words, and he leaned forward as he asked his next question. "Really? That sounds pretty promising as far as your new business goes, doesn't it?"

Haley hesitated for a fraction of a second before admitting, "I guess so. The work he needs done is right up my alley."

"That sounds great, honey," her father enthused.

Mrs. Jordenson returned just then, carrying three plates of mincemeat pie, her husband's favorite.

"What's so great?" she asked jovially. "My cooking, I hope."

"Haley was just telling me that she's gotten a fantastic offer to work on the latest Sullivan restaurant. Where did you say it was, Haley?"

"In Canada. But—"

"Canada," her mother breathed, distributing the plates of pie and then taking her seat. "It's *so* lovely there. What a perfect place to start off your career."

"Now, wait a minute." Haley held up a hand, calling a halt to this runaway discussion about her nonexistent future as art consultant for the Sullivan

43

chain. "I didn't say a thing about going to work for Lance Sullivan. I only mentioned to Dad that Lance asked me about the possibility of taking care of his newest Canadian restaurant. But I turned him down."

Mr. Jordenson's face altered drastically at this piece of obviously unexpected news. "For God's sake, Haley, why did you do that? It's not as though you have a backlog of offers awaiting your attention."

"No, it's true, I don't," Haley answered, taken aback at her father's apparent anger over the matter. "But I'm sure," she went on carefully, "it's just a matter of patience on my part. I've made lots of contacts this past week, and some of them seemed quite interested in using my services."

"Yes, dear, I'm sure that's true," Mrs. Jordenson inserted. "But why give up such a lucrative offer? You can't afford to be picky now. Not at the very start of your career."

"Damn right," Mr. Jordenson put in. "When I was first starting out in the construction business, do you think I turned down the first offer I received? Hell, no! I took all sorts of jobs. Anything and everything I could get my hands on. If someone would have offered me a job like the one Lance Sullivan offered you, I would have grabbed it!"

Ernest clenched one of his fists to emphasize his last words, and it suddenly dawned on Haley that he was taking this matter far more personally than was necessary. Slowly she reached for her plate of pie and began to toy with it absently.

"Dad," she began quietly, "why don't you tell me what you're really getting at?"

Glancing up, she noticed a flicker of uncertainty cross her father's solid features, fading rapidly as he appeared to have made up his mind about something.

"All right," he said, his shoulders relaxing visibly as he leaned back in his chair.

"Ernest, don't you think—" her mother piped up, only to be waved back into silence by her husband.

"Never mind, Rita," Mr. Jordenson said. "We shouldn't be keeping this from her."

"What in the world are you two talking about?" Haley asked, startled at her father's admission that there really was something to all this.

"If you'll just listen, I'll tell you," Mr. Jordenson said. When Haley made no attempt to say anything more, he continued. "Your mother and I knew about Lance's asking you to work for him on his new restaurant. In fact, it's because of me that he asked you."

Haley's amber eyes widened in amazement, but she kept quiet, waiting for her father to continue his story.

"Now, you know I've been associated with Lance's father, George, for a hell of a long time. Ever since we first moved to Littleton and I got started in the construction business, in fact. Hell's bells, if it wasn't for me, the Sullivan business wouldn't have had a chance of getting started here in the Denver area. Things were tough back then; just acquiring the materials to start up a new business called for a downright miracle."

Haley nodded. She knew by heart the story her

father was expounding. She had heard the story of George Sullivan's struggle to the top many times, always finding it interesting, no matter how many times he'd related the familiar yarn. Right now, however, she hoped her father would skim over most of it and get to the point.

George Sullivan, her father reiterated, in his meteoric rise to the pinnacle of the restaurant business, had acquired a rather snobbish attitude over the years, quickly forgetting those who'd lent him a helping hand up the ladder of success. That fact had always been a thorn in Ernest Jordenson's side, although not until today had Haley been aware of the extent of his resentment.

In his roundabout way Haley's father revealed that having failed all these years to teach the high and mighty George Sullivan a thing or two, he'd decided the time had come for the fellow to own up to his past debts. Ernest had cornered him at a recent Chamber of Commerce meeting, informing him that his daughter was going into business for herself. He'd pointedly indicated that her skills as an art consultant would be helpful to George's son, Lance, who had taken over most of the management responsibilities of the chain. George had obviously taken the not too subtle hint, and Ernest was pleased as punch by his successful ruse.

It was achingly apparent to Haley that her refusal of the job would complicate her father's carefully thought out scheme to even the score with his old business associate.

"Dad, I—I don't know what to say," Haley began after her father finished his story. Indeed, she didn't.

46

What in the world was she going to do about all this now? Her parents knew nothing about her affair with Lance before he'd married Julia—and they would certainly never learn of it from Haley's lips. How could she explain that that was the real reason for her not wanting to work for the man? Obviously there was no way the truth of the matter could come out.

"Now, Haley," her father was saying, "I know you want to be able to say that you got started completely on your own. I'm sure the idea of nepotism doesn't sit well with you. But, honey, you can wait a long time for things to happen if you let pride rule your entire life."

To a certain extent, her father was right in his assessment of her feelings. Haley did possess a tremendous amount of pride when it came to accomplishing things on her own, and it was harder for her than most people to accept help from others. But in this case pride was the least important factor in her reticence. The fact that her parents chose to believe it was, however, an unexpected out as far as having to make further explanations went.

"I guess you're right, Dad," Haley said. "I certainly haven't made any progress on my own this week." She sighed, emphasizing her disappointment somewhat more than she felt it. The wheels were clicking in her brain, though, and it didn't take long for her to come to the conclusion that if this whole thing meant so much to her father, then there was simply no other choice for her but to go along with his wishes and accept the job, regardless of Lance. She would do anything to keep from upsetting her father in his present physical condition, including working

47

for the man she had once vowed would have nothing to do with her life ever again. So much for resolutions, she mused wryly.

"The thing is," Haley added, "the job would involve going to Canada. Maybe just before Christmas."

"But so what, honey?" her mother asked, eyes brightening as she recognized her daughter's apparent relenting. She, too, would have done anything for her husband, and if it pleased him to get back at old George Sullivan, she'd help all she could. "Think how much fun you would have. Greta said it's positively fantastic there—you might even get a chance to do some skiing."

"That's true," Haley agreed. "In fact, the restaurant is in Banff. Isn't that where Greta and Sam and the girls stayed a few years ago?"

"Why, yes—of course, it is," her mother answered, smiling broadly. "Now, Haley, dear, I don't want to sound like the typical meddlesome mother, but I think you'll be making a serious mistake if you don't go. Not with all you're being offered."

Haley peered at her mother beneath half-closed lids, then slanted her gaze to her father; his expression suggested he was smugly confident that he'd already won his case. She shook her auburn head and clicked her tongue reprovingly.

"You guys are a couple of nuts," she teased. "Sneaking around and plotting behind my back."

"I don't call it plotting," Mr. Jordenson objected lightly, cutting into his pie enthusiastically now that the subject was settled. "I call it careful, constructive planning."

48

They all chuckled, Haley allowing herself to forget for the moment exactly what she had just let herself in for.

Later that evening, after returning to her town house, Haley's thoughts about the pleasant evening she'd spent in her parents' company gave way to the problem she was now facing. What was she going to do? She'd told her father she would accept Lance's offer, but a week had passed since she'd last spoken to him, a week in which he could have already hired someone else for the job.

But no, that wouldn't make sense if the only reason he'd offered it in the first place was to appease his father. Haley's face took on a derisive expression. What an act the man had put on, pretending he was asking because of her undeniable talent! Hogwash! He probably would have never even asked her if it hadn't been for his father's prodding.

Haley sighed, searching through the kitchen cupboard, where she kept the telephone book. It was all water under the bridge anyway, she thought, knowing she'd have to get in touch with Lance and let him know she wanted the position.

She was somewhat surprised to hear his voice on the other end of the line. After all, it was almost ten o'clock on Friday night. She'd have thought he'd be out socializing or checking up on one of his restaurants.

"Well, hello there," he greeted her warmly. "I didn't think I'd be hearing from you."

"I didn't think I'd be calling," Haley replied, a

touch caustically. "But I've changed my mind about the job offer."

"Oh? Why is that?"

Haley bit her tongue, forcing back the sarcastic reply she'd like to give him. *Because I'm doing this for my father.*

"I need the work," she stated tersely. Well, *that* was true enough. She was tired of making the rounds, touting her as yet untapped skills. It would be nice to put those skills to work again.

"Is the position still open?" she asked.

"Yes. As a matter of fact, it is." Lance hesitated, then added, "Let me ask you. How soon could you be ready to leave for Banff?"

"Well. . . . I suppose as soon as you need me," Haley answered, mentally reeling off all the pre-Christmas shopping she had not as yet done. It was unlike her to wait until the last few weeks to shop, but this year things had been so hectic, she hadn't had time for anything except moving back home and starting her new business.

"Good," Lance said, "because I'd like for you to leave next week. I'd like to open the restaurant shortly after New Year's—possibly even New Year's Eve. So it's important that you get started right away."

Stunned by the news that Lance wanted her to leave so soon, Haley said nothing for a moment. "All right," she agreed quietly.

"I'll make all the arrangements concerning your flight and hotel accommodations, so there's no need for you to worry about any of that. I suppose . . . there really isn't that much time. Hmmm."

"Time for what?" Haley asked.

"We need to get together to go over the details of what I want before you leave. When would be a good time for you in the next couple of days?"

"I—I suppose tomorrow," Haley said, her mind still reacting in confusion to this sudden turn of events.

"That sounds good," Lance said, all crisp efficiency now. "How about dinner tomorrow night? I can pick you up at your place."

"No," Haley responded quickly. "I—I don't think that would be such a good time for me. But. . . . I could meet you somewhere for lunch if you like."

"Sounds all right," Lance said; nodding. Haley thought she detected a note of amusement in his voice, and his attitude rankled her.

"How about Professor Plum's?" Lance suggested.

"Not one of your own?"

"It doesn't hurt to visit the competetion as often as opportunity allows," Lance explained dryly. "What time is convenient for you?"

"Oh, I suppose one o'clock."

"All right," Lance agreed. "I'll see you then. And Haley . . ."

"Yes?"

"I'm happy you decided to take the job."

Haley swallowed deeply. "Yes, well, good night." Lance bid her good night, and after placing the receiver in its cradle, she sat staring at it for several moments, thoroughly chagrined that her thus far well kept resolution of total uninvolvement with Lance Sullivan had been so quickly dissolved.

Well, she thought, sighing resignedly, it just

couldn't be helped. She'd promised her father she'd take the job, and she had gone through with it. And it wouldn't be that traumatic just working for Lance, would it? It wasn't as though she'd be working side by side with him. That was one thing she intended to make clear from the start, she noted mentally. After ascertaining just exactly what he had in mind for the new restaurant, she'd take full charge of the detail work involved. She might as well get started on the right foot in this new venture, and if she could manage to secure personal control of the project from the very beginning, then future problems could be more easily averted.

The decision was a morale booster, one she sorely needed before facing up to the real nerve-tester she was to face tomorrow—meeting with Lance again.

Haley and Lance were seated at a heavy oak table cozily nestled in one corner of Professor Plum's many subdued, cleverly decorated rooms. An abundance of exotic plants seeming to grow from every available space surrounded them, creating a verdant cage of privacy.

"So you enjoyed Philadelphia?" Lance was saying, as casually as though she had merely been gone on a short out-of-town trip. Haley squirmed uncomfortably as the wide sensuous mouth she had once known so intimately spread into a familiar grin.

"Yes, as a matter of fact, I did," Haley replied. "It was a great experience. I learned a lot."

Lance cocked an eyebrow skeptically. "Is that so? Like what?"

Haley's composure sizzled beneath the flaming intensity of Lance's gaze, and it was a struggle to keep her tone even. "Oh, you know," she answered, waving a hand nonchalantly, "all about living alone, working for a big firm. All sorts of things."

"Men, for instance," Lance suggested dryly.

Haley flushed deeply, angry with herself for being so easily baited. "That's really none of your business," she stated brusquely, then lifted her glass of ice water to her lips, the cool liquid sliding mercifully down her parched throat.

Lance leaned back in his chair, crossing both arms over his chest, studying her reaction with a self-satisfied expression. His smugness rankled Haley; she'd be damned if she'd put up with this ridiculous cat-and-mouse game.

Producing a plastic smile, Haley said, "Why don't we get to the point, Lance? When is it you want me to leave?"

His reply was slow in coming; Haley could sense his reluctance to get down to business. Nevertheless she held his gaze unwaveringly.

"Next Wednesday," he said finally. "Can you handle that?"

"Of course."

"Good. Here's what I want."

Much to Haley's grateful satisfaction most of the conversation for the next hour and a half centered on Lance's ideas for his Banff restaurant. Haley would be staying at the Banff Springs Hotel, the same one her sister had spoken so highly of before. She'd be working beside Mike Lindquist, the young man Lance had hired as manager, but basically she'd be on her own as far as any decisions to be made concerning the various art acquisitions she thought appropriate to Lance's scheme.

Fairly pleased with the outcome of the dreaded luncheon, Haley walked alongside Lance as they left the restaurant. The afternoon sun was slipping slowly along a brilliant blue western horizon; the temperature was cold but crisp and refreshing. Haley's spirits had taken a decided upswing with the prospect of genuine, much-needed work waiting to be tackled—regardless of the client.

"Where is your car?" Lance asked as they strolled down the brick pathway that branched off toward a tiny parking lot in back of the restaurant.

"Just up the street," Haley answered. She stopped and reached inside her purse for her sunglasses. She slipped them on, reducing the sun's glare, and secured her clutch bag beneath her arm.

"Which way?" Lance asked.

"To the left, but—" Haley had taken a few steps, then stopped. Evidently Lance had intended to follow her.

"Come on, I'll walk with you," Lance interrupted, and the objection she had been about to voice died on her lips. What difference did it make anyway? She wouldn't be seeing him again for a while.

Haley stopped on the sidewalk next to her burnt orange Audi and reached inside her clutch bag for her keys. As she did so, her elbow touched the sleeve of Lance's tweed jacket. Thinking he was behind her, she was startled by his nearness and reacted as though a volt of electricity had suddenly arced through her arm. Determined to hide her embarrassment, she moved briskly forward, bending slightly as she slid the key inside the door to unlock the Audi.

"So," she said, slightly breathless, removing her sunglasses as she turned back to face him, "will I be hearing from you before next Wednesday?" A barely perceptible breeze lifted a lock of auburn hair, tossing it across one cheek. Automatically Haley reached up to pull it away, but the motion was intercepted as Lance's hand suddenly grabbed her own, grasping it in midair.

"Don't." The quiet husky tone of the command riddled Haley to the core; the physical contact alone was almost overwhelming as a host of never forgotten responses seemed to enervate every synapse in her body. Unable to move, she was barely aware of the shallow rapidity of her breathing as Lance's cool gray-green gaze pinned her to the spot, studying every centimeter of her face, forehead, cheeks, lips, rediscovering in detail what his own lips had once possessed so completely.

Gently Lance's fingertips removed the stray lock of hair, smoothing it against the side of her head, his hand softly crushing the silken auburn tresses. Haley's eyes seemed riveted to his strong square chin; every possible defense she would have summoned was momentarily conquered by the traitorous responses of her body to this man.

With measured deliberation Lance's thumb traced a pattern along the outer edge of Haley's face, down the slightly prominent cheekbone, along the ridge of her jawline, resting finally at the corner of her mouth. With feather lightness his thumb slid across the velvet softness of her lips, the back and forth motion forcing them apart, allowing his thumb access to the inner contours of her mouth and the hardness of her white teeth.

Haley drew in a sharp breath, her heart thumping erratically as the rest of her body reacted wildly to the intimacy of Lance's touch. *This is ridiculous!* some inner voice screamed in objection. Yet, the saner, more experienced part of her knew that indeed, it was only normal that she should be responding as if Lance were actually kissing her now, as deeply and fully as if their lips and tongues were already joined together in fiery reunion. Hadn't he always had this much power over her? How could she have been so naive as to believe she could ever develop an immunity to it?

With tremendous soul-wrenching resolve, Haley reached up and removed his hand. Unconsciously she bit her lower lip, then her upper one, as if to erase the imprint of his thumb. "I—you didn't answer my question," she faltered, turning quickly and opening the car door.

"I'll be in touch," Lance said smoothly, stepping back a bit as Haley slid inside the car. After she shut the door, he leaned forward, both hands resting on the upper door frame as he answered, "I'll have my secretary take care of the airline tickets and hotel reservations, as well as anything else you might need."

"All right," Haley said, replacing her sunglasses and switching on the ignition. "Thank you for the lunch," she added, incredibly grateful as he removed his hands from the car and stepped back. The closeness of him still clung to her with a smothering intensity. She had to get away from him. Immediately. As Lance bade her good-bye, it was all she could do to keep her foot steady as it bore down on the accelerator.

An image of her father's face appeared before her, bringing back to mind the reason that had propelled her into the untenable position she found herself in today, the reaction to which gripped her even now. Had she perhaps stretched her loyalty to her father to the absolute limits?

A question, Haley mused wryly, she hoped would never have to be answered.

CHAPTER FOUR

The next few days were a flurry of constant activity. Haley managed to get in some shopping, and although most of it pertained to her own needs, she did manage to work in a few items on her list for her family. On Monday morning she spoke briefly with Lance, their conversation rather formal.

There was nothing further either one of them needed to say concerning her trip anyway. But her feelings about the whole thing were mixed. The scene at Professor Plum's had shaken Haley considerably —she still hadn't recovered from it. Firmly she reminded herself of her father's wishes and pushed aside for the umpteenth time the disturbing emotions churning inside her. The one saving factor, for which she was overwhelmingly grateful, was that she would be handling the project alone—without Lance. Thank God for that, Haley thought.

On Tuesday she picked up her airline tickets and bus reservations at the travel agency Lance had used, and she was surprised to discover that she'd been booked on a charter flight instead of a commercial one. By Tuesday night she was flying around the town house a mile a minute, making last-minute phone calls, and packing up everything she hoped would be necessary for the trip. Too keyed up to sleep, she could manage only a few hours that night, but felt surprisingly refreshed the next morning.

The chartered airplane was completely filled, and

to Haley's dismay, as soon as it was airborne the plane was transformed into one of the most enormous, hell-raising, everyone-join-in parties that she'd ever witnessed. At first she was appalled by the raucous laughing and singing, and the inordinate amount of drinking among virtually every one of the passengers, but soon she decided that, since there was no means of escape, she might as well enjoy herself along with the rest.

As the airplane began its descent into Calgary International Airport, the volume aboard the aircraft became decibels lower, and Haley was relieved at the opportunity to lie back and try to rest a little before what was bound to be a hectic scramble for luggage and the correct bus—especially among this boisterous group, who were all headed in the same direction as she was.

The late afternoon sun seemed to melt over the countryside through which the bus was traveling, gilding the breathtaking landscape with a warm, buttery glow. Haley kept her eyes glued to the frigid windowpane, taking in mile after mile of snow-covered Rocky Mountain terrain, blinking in surprise at the occasional glimpses of bighorn sheep, lumbering moose, soft-eyed deer, and more infrequently, the majestic, sure-footed mountain goats that roamed the rocky crags.

Though interesting and enjoyable in many respects, the bus ride was a long one. Haley's companion was an amiable, garulous woman in her mid-fifties. She had been here several times before, and Haley listened appreciatively at the wealth of information the woman spewed forth about this wonderful part of North America.

Nighttime was settling its darkening blanket around the small village of Banff as the bus passed within the city limits, but as it rolled slowly through the busy downtown streets Haley was glad they were arriving at this particular time of day. Christmas lights and colorful decorations glimmered everywhere, creating a tinsel town of the cozy shops and restaurants lining Banff Avenue; customers and patrons bustled about on their way home or headed toward an evening of dining and nightclubbing. Haley wondered briefly where the new Sullivan's was located, but the thought was brought up sharp as the bus began slowing down at what appeared to be the entrance to the Banff Springs Hotel grounds. The driver's subsequent announcement confirmed the supposition.

As the bus wended its way through the long, curving drive, the enormous, skybound pines created a surrealistic effect of some secluded fairy-tale forest. What awaited the curious passengers at the end of the drive, however, brought gasps of delight and wonder from them all. Haley, like the rest of the passengers, was totally stunned by the magnificence of the enormous structure standing before them.

She had read in the brochures provided by the travel agency that the hotel was a replica of a Scottish castle in Banffshire, Scotland, erected during the 1920s. It was an enormous thing, the multilayered complex larger than anything her imagination could have fathomed. The overwhelming impression it presented was one of a perfect residence for the royalty

of olden days—one could imagine knights and la-
dies-in-waiting ensconced within the protective stone
walls. Stepping outside the bus, Haley bid her companion good-bye and waited as most of the other
passengers disembarked and headed toward the massive oak doors of the hotel's front entrance.

Pulling her stylish sheepskin coat tightly around
her, Haley followed slowly, her head swiveling as she
took it all in, completely awestruck with the fascinating surroundings that were to be her home away
from home for a while.

Haley immediately recognized the fact that staying in such a charming setting could add immensely
to the atmosphere she would need to absorb in order
to create the proper style Lance was seeking in his
new restaurant. She had the distinct feeling that it
wasn't going to be such a difficult chore.

Inside, after waiting in line at the front desk, Haley
finally obtained the key to her room. Locating her
luggage among the abundant assortment scattered
about the slate floor of the lobby took longer than
she'd expected, but having finally accomplished that,
she secured a porter, who led her toward the elevators. Within minutes she was on her way up to her
room, listening with delight to the melodious French
chattering of the young female elevator operator as
she conversed with some of the other people aboard.
It appeared that all of the youthful kilt-clad employees Haley had observed so far were fluent in both
English and French.

Her room, she discovered, was truly delightful. It
was a simple affair: a pastel blue carpet that matched
the more muted shade of the walls, a maple dressing

61

table and armoire, and a small table with two comfortable-looking chairs situated next to the single French window. Impulsively Haley unlatched it, the doors swinging outward, their bottoms almost scraping the snowy surface of the rooftop they opened onto.

The room was chilly, but the rush of cold air was refreshing, and Haley had visions of what it must look like in the morning. Suddenly shivering, she shut the window and opened up the valve on the radiator. Crossing the room, she opened the door to a surprisingly large bathroom, fascinated at once with the oversize claw-footed bathtub and solid brass appointments.

Opening the taps and adjusting them to the right temperature, she left the bathroom, swinging the largest of her suitcases onto the bed to begin unpacking. A blinking light on the telephone caught her attention, and she crossed the room to where it stood on the bedside table, picking up the black receiver and dialing the number for the front desk.

"May I help you?" the desk clerk answered.

"Yes, please," Haley answered. "This is Room Four Thirty-nine, Haley Jordenson. I forgot to ask when I checked in. Do I have any messages?"

"Just a moment, please, and I'll check." Haley waited while the clerk put her on hold. "Yes. There is a note from a Mr. Michael Lindquist. He left a number for you to call as soon as you arrived."

"Oh, good. May I have it, please?"

First things first, Haley thought, after jotting the number down. She removed her clothing and other articles from the suitcase and began placing them in various drawers of the dresser. Gathering a soft flannel nightgown and the familiar terry-cloth robe, she entered the bathroom, ready to indulge herself in a nice long hot soak.

Afterward she glanced at the travel alarm clock she'd remembered to bring along and decided nine thirty certainly wasn't too late to call Mike Lindquist. A few moments later she had him on the line, and after a brief friendly discussion in which they both agreed to a time in the morning when they could meet, Haley felt satisfied that the man sounded like a reasonable person, one she might even enjoy working with.

Her first impression proved completely accurate, Haley discovered the next morning when Mike came to pick her up in his car. Mike Lindquist was a truly amicable young man in his late twenties—the perfect sort to manage Lance's new venture, Haley decided. An athletic type, he indicated his enjoyment of skiing and various other outdoor activities, but seemed to be as determined as his boss to make the new Sullivan's stand out in the small though tremendously popular resort town of Banff. After talking to him only a short while, Haley had no doubt that Mike could pull it off.

"Where do you live, Mike?" Haley asked. She was dividing her attention at the moment between their conversation and the city sights that looked so different from last night's appearance. Mike maneuvered the car slowly and carefully down the snow- and ice-encrusted streets, giving Haley a chance to soak it all in. The restaurant, she discovered, was located on the opposite side of the town from the hotel.

"Right now I'm renting a house," Mike answered. "I'd like to buy something, but it's rare that anything ever comes on the market around these parts." He lifted one shoulder expressively, tiny lines fanning out from the corners of his eyes as his tanned face broke out in an unaffected grin. "But I can wait. I plan on being around long enough to grab the first one that becomes available."

As they entered the parking lot, which offered Haley her first glimpse of the restaurant, he said, "Well, here we are." He hesitated, watching Haley's expression before adding, "So what do you think of it?"

Haley's amber eyes widened as she took in the strikingly attractive building ahead of them.

"It's marvelous," she gushed. "Really. Most of the Sullivan's I've seen are unique, but this one is definitely the most impressive."

"Wait till you see the inside," Mike said, parking the car close to the front entrance of the building.

Opening her door, Haley stepped out, eyeing the contemporary structure with more than simple admiration. She had to hand it to Lance, she admitted silently. This was his finest to date. No wonder he referred to the place as his pet project.

The restaurant used the surrounding landscape to its fullest advantage. An expertly designed conglomeration of free-flowing angles, the restaurant's natural wood exterior blended beautifully with the verdant lushness of the pine and cedar forest within which it was nestled. Tinted glass windows were abundant, creating an almost fishbowl effect from the inside.

Mike unlocked the front door, and Haley walked ahead of him into the brick-floored entry hall. The crisp newness of the place was evident in the pleasant smell of wood and fresh paint. As Mike flipped on the lights, Haley began her tour of the entire restaurant, her mind already teeming with ideas for the approach she was going to take to create a proper artistic scheme.

Mike walked alongside her, guiding her through the maze of dining rooms that were virtually completed.

"As you can see," Mike said, gesturing with one hand, "the place is just waiting for your final touches."

Haley drew in an invigorating breath and exhaled slowly, turning and studying the room in which they were standing with a critical eye.

"Well," she said, smiling, "I'm ready to get started."

"Let me show you where my office is located," Mike offered. "I've an extra desk that is at your disposal."

"Great," Haley enthused, following Mike as he led the way back down the main corridor and up a flight of stairs just opposite the kitchen.

Half an hour later she was seated comfortably at her desk in Mike's spacious, cheery office, organizing the mass of booklets and catalogs that had filled her briefcase to almost overflowing.

Haley settled in to her first job with an enthusiasm that surpassed anything else she'd ever done. Thoughts of Lance and Julia and the complications she'd left behind were readily shoved to the back of her mind. Regardless of the real reason for her being offered the position, she couldn't have been anything but grateful for the chance. The work was interesting and a definite learning experience, and would get her new career off to an impressive start.

The following two days were consumed in a whirl-wind of ferocious decision making and telephone calls, and by Friday evening she was more than casually receptive to Mike's invitation to join him for supper at a small restaurant in town specializing in Italian food. Haley felt very much at ease with the young man, sensing that he regarded their relationship as nothing more than a professional one, although it could easily develop, given time, she decided, into a genuine friendship.

Haley happily accepted an invitation to accompany Mike and some of his friends to Sunshine Mountain Saturday morning. She set her alarm for an early wake-up, giving herself enough time to enjoy breakfast and then get into her bulky ski gear. By nine thirty she was waiting at the circular drive at the back of the massive hotel, where buses departed for the half-hour journeys to the three available mountains. A short while later Mike drove up, parking his car in the adjacent lot.

While waiting for the ten o'clock bus, Mike introduced Haley to the others: Scott was a free-lance ski instructor in Banff for the season, and Sherrie and Beth—both women about Haley's age—were working their way through the ski season as waitresses in one of the local restaurants. Mike had promised them both jobs at Sullivan's as soon as it opened.

Early snows had created an impressive base for all

three mountains, but recent falls had blessed the slopes of Sunshine Mountain with even more of the powdery substance. Haley was an advanced skiier, and kept up handily with the others. By early afternoon, however, she began to feel the effects of the strenuous activity, and begged off for the rest of the open lifttime.

Tired and somewhat sleepy, Haley leaned her head against the cold window of the bus, her half-closed eyes taking in the fascinating scenery she had observed earlier.

Upon returning to her room and ridding herself of every vestige of clothing, she fell into bed, her body giving in to her brain's demands by rapidly drifting off into a sound, heavy sleep.

Her eyes fluttered open as the musical sound of a bird's chirping on the outside rooftop penetrated her consciousness. Disoriented, Haley had to think for a moment where she was, the room having become darkened in the evening hour. She arched her back and stretched her taut, overworked limbs, her mouth contorting in a long, deliciously uninhibited yawn.

Her stomach growled with hunger, but somehow the thought of food was not uppermost in her mind; neither was the work she'd set up for herself in the coming week. The closest she could come to defining the feeling she was experiencing at the moment was perhaps a touch of melancholy—which was strange, Haley thought, since she couldn't have been more satisfied with the way things were turning out.

Perhaps it was because Christmas was just around the corner and she missed sharing the festive atmosphere with those she knew and loved. True, she'd spent a lovely day with a really fun and likable group of people, and she'd seemed to fit right in with them. She certainly was not lacking for company while she was here.

So what was the problem? she wondered, amazed that she suddenly felt choked up, her eyes moistening with the threat of tears. Never one to overanalyze her feelings or give in to depression for very long, she wiped away with the back of one hand the one droplet that had managed to escape.

Determined to get her mind on other things, she sat up and leaned over to switch on the bedside lamp. Eight o'clock! She stared at the lighted clock in complete bewilderment. She must have been really tired to have slept four hours without waking even once.

The rumble in her stomach grew to downright demanding proportions, so after flipping through the printed hotel menu, Haley placed her order with room service, getting up and taking a hasty shower before the food arrived.

The unexpected emotional episode was pushed to the farthest recesses of her mind as she spent the rest of the evening poring over publisher's catalogs of current in-stock graphics and brochures of local galleries that she planned on visiting in the next week. The glass of wine she'd ordered to accompany her meal was soothing and relaxing, and a couple of hours later Haley put everything away and crawled back into bed. It was obvious that she was overtired from working at such a hectic pace, which could very well account for her unusual fatigue and mild depression.

She awoke the next morning to observe a light

snowfall: feathery flakes pattered against the windowpanes. She'd made no specific plans for the day, so she rolled over and closed her eyes again, drifting off into a half sleep. Waking was much easier the second time she attempted it, and as she pushed back the covers Haley stood up, stretched her arms high above her head, and padded across the soft carpeting toward the bathroom. She had just placed her hand on the doorknob when something small and white lying just inside the door caught her attention.

Looping her hair behind one ear, Haley bent to scoop up the folded piece of paper. Opening it, she read the hasty scrawl, then reread it, her mouth parting in stunned amazement at the signature.

> Got in last night. Am on my way to breakfast in the main dining room. Join me there when you get up.
>
> Lance.

What in the world? Haley wondered, completely shocked. Lance was here! In this same hotel. It couldn't be, she told herself. He'd assured her that she would be working solo on this project, with help, of course, if need be, from Mike Lindquist.

The telltale flip of her heart, however, revealed more clearly than she would have liked to admit, that she was not as displeased as she should have been at this sudden turn of events. She knew as surely as anything that the last person she needed to see was Lance Sullivan. Then how to explain this sudden flurry of activity she felt compelled to engage in? She was behaving like some slavegirl responding to her master's beck and call.

Face-scrubbing was accomplished quickly, the toothpaste lid was screwed back on, and she was applying a daytime ration of makeup to her delicately angular porcelain features. Securing her hair in a topknot, she rid herself of her bathrobe and slipped into a pair of designer jeans and a mauve cashmere sweater.

Only after she was inside the creaking elevator, slowly making its descent to the lobby level, did Haley manage to compose herself. But her heart still tripped at a ridiculous rate as she covered the distance to the main dining room, widened amber orbs scanning the room's breakfast patrons, a virtual battle of emotions warring within her breast as she searched the crowded room for Lance.

He was seated near the farthest wall, next to the window, sipping at a cup of coffee as he read a newspaper. Even from here she could discern the broad expanse of his shoulders, tufts of toasted brown hair curling down across the neckline of the blue and green ski sweater he wore.

As she walked toward him, making her way among the white linen-covered tables, the clinking sounds of glasses and silverware and the bustling waiters made absolutely no impression on her. The quivering, jellylike sensation in the pit of her stomach was the only physical reality she was aware of. In a flash she realized the full import of her depression the night before. She'd been on her own a great deal these past couple of years, but there was something about the loveliness of this fairy-tale place that made one seem incomplete without some sort of companionship.

"Hello, Lance," Haley greeted him, knowing in the second it took for his ruggedly carved features to break their absorption with the newspaper and turn to face her, that for some inexplicable reason her world here no longer felt incomplete.

"Good morning," Lance returned the greeting, smiling broadly as he stood and pulled out a chair for her.

"I must say, this is quite a surprise," Haley said, giving her head a small shake. "I had no idea you were coming. As I understood it, I was to be handling this job on my own."

Lance folded the newspaper and laid it down on the table. "And you will be." One eyebrow lifted as he added somewhat mockingly, "My interest in the restaurant extends to other things besides the artwork I'm going to invest in."

Haley's cheeks warmed with a tinge of embarrassment. "I'm sure it does," she answered tightly. "I thought perhaps you might have had an attack of doubt concerning my ability to handle things."

"There's no need to become defensive," Lance said quietly. His cool hazel gaze held hers for a thoughtful moment. "I have no doubt whatsoever of your ability. I trust you implicitly to create the proper atmosphere for the restaurant."

Haley cocked her head and winced derisively.

"You can stop the game, Lance," she said. "I know exactly why you hired me for this job, and it doesn't have a damn thing to do with my qualifications."

71

Lance's brows shot upward bemusedly. "What are you talking about?" he asked.

Haley rolled her eyes upward. "Is this necessary? Really, Lance, you know and I know that the only reason you were even interested in taking me on was because of my father prevailing upon yours for an overdue return of favor."

Lance sat back and regarded her coolly. "I see. You think my dad is the puppeteer and I merely dance when he pulls the strings, is that it?"

"Not exactly. But I would guess that he still maintains some control in the family enterprise."

"You're right about that," Lance conceded. "And —I'll admit that he was the first to bring up the matter of hiring you."

"Well," Haley said wryly, "at last I've heard it. You can finally admit that you were more or less pushed into it. I'm sure you couldn't care less about my qualifications."

The waiter arrived with menus and poured a fresh cup of coffee for Lance, Haley indicating with a nod that she would care for a cup also.

"Why don't we order breakfast?" Lance suggested smoothly, ignoring her last gibe. "That way we'll have more energy to pursue this terrifically interesting subject."

"Why not?" Haley answered gamely, a corner of her full lips lifting upward in an aloof smile. Actually she would be much more at ease engaging in another bantering conversation with Lance. It would successfully veil, she hoped, from both Lance and herself, the emotional turmoil still churning inside her, the result, as always, of his mere presence.

72

After a while, however, Haley began to relax somewhat, allowing Lance to lead her into a far more pleasant discussion of what had happened since her arrival a few days earlier.

"I have an appointment at a publisher's house in Calgary on Monday," Haley informed him, placing her knife and fork down on her now empty plate. "They have an impressive list of graphics that I think would fit in very well with what I have in mind. Tuesday I had planned on visiting a small gallery here. I'd like to see what kind of works are available by local artists. Hopefully I'll be able to use some of them."

"Sounds as though you've really got the ball rolling," Lance commented approvingly. "I was planning on driving over and checking things out at the restaurant this morning. Would you like to come with me?"

Haley hesitated for the briefest moment before answering, "All right. It will give me the opportunity to show you what I'm talking about."

Lance glanced at his wristwatch and then back at Haley.

"Can you be ready in thirty minutes?"

"I'm ready now," Haley said. "All I have to do is go back to my room for my coat."

Lance stood, moving around the table to place a

hand on the back of Haley's chair. "I'll meet you in the lobby in a few minutes then."

Haley agreed, and together the two of them left the restaurant, Lance saying he wanted to visit the hotel's gift shop to purchase a roll of film, and Haley walking on toward the elevators.

The dense gray cast of the sky had lightened considerably, an indication of possibly fairer weather.

"I hope the weather clears up for my trip to Calgary," Haley commented, speaking her thoughts aloud.

"Mike gave you the use of his car, I presume," Lance inquired.

"Yes, he did," Haley said. "I'm grateful for that. It's a good thing he has another one at his disposal. I think he would have gotten tired of having to shuttle me around while I'm here."

"What do you think of him?" Lance asked. He turned the wheel into the parking lot of the restaurant, his gray-green gaze surveying all that had been accomplished in his absence.

"Mike? I don't think you could have chosen a more loyal or capable manager," Haley said, adding, "He's very likable and easy to work with."

"Good. I thought you'd think just that." Lance reached for the door handle and Haley did the same, stepping outside the car onto the crunchy newly fallen snow that had covered everything in a smooth white blanket.

Inside, Haley removed her coat and stomped her boots against the floor grating, clumps of caked snow breaking off and falling through the metal slits.

"Brrr," she muttered, rubbing her hands together

briskly, as she followed Lance into the main hallway. "It's colder than I'd expected."

"Mmm-hmm," Lance agreed, taking up the familiar stance of one fisted hand on his hip, his squarish jaw jutting forward as his attention became riveted to the details of the restaurant.

Noticing his almost immediate preoccupation, Haley said, "I think I'll go on upstairs."

Lance nodded, and she quietly moved past him and down the corridor. She'd decided it would be a good idea to at least give Lance an idea of the general scheme she had in mind. Now that he was here, she realized it was really for the best. She'd much rather suffer his disapproval of her final selections before than after the fact. Letting herself in the office, she went directly to her desk, shuffling among the folders in search of one containing the preliminary sketches she'd made to help determine appropriate selections later at both the gallery and publisher's house. So absorbed was she in the task that she was completely unaware of the opening and closing of the door followed by footsteps moving in her direction.

Not until Lance was close behind her, the woodsy fragrance of his after-shave invading her physical awareness, did she turn, startled that he was standing so near to her—only inches away. His stare was of an intensity that immediately put her on her guard, his eyes barely disguising the lustful yearnings she remembered all too well.

Swallowing spasmodically, Haley thrust out the papers she was now clenching in one hand, creating a barrier, however flimsy, between the two of them.

"I—you startled me," she faltered, managing a

wavering smile. "I was searching my desk for this proposal. I thought it might give you a better idea of wha—" Her words evaporated as Lance took the folder from her hand and placed it on the desk behind her.

Haley fought desperately for words of protest as Lance's hands grasped her shoulders, pulling her closely against his lean hardness, but her mind refused to cooperate, unwilling to formulate the simplest sentence.

Her eyes, too, remained unwilling to face the raw need in his own; she closed them as his warm breath fanned out across her cheeks. Quietly his lips descended upon hers, their fiery touch at once searing yet gentle, knowlegeable yet curious as they melded their brand into her. All at once the passion she had spent night after sleepless night trying desperately to forget came rushing back in a soul-shaking assault on her senses.

He must have noted her body's melting response as she slumped against him, unable to support her own weight. Deftly Lance's hands left her shoulders, sliding lown the length of her back to grasp firmly the sides of her trim waist. As he pushed his weight against hers, Haley felt the edge of the table pressing on the backs of her thighs, forcing her into a half-sitting position.

Instinctively her arms found their way beneath his, her hands sliding upward across the rough material of his sweater, fingers splaying out and pressing deeply into the hard, taut, muscular back. Without any further pursuasion from Lance her lips parted, the inner flesh of his mouth and the velvet roughness of his tongue meeting her own, rekindling the fire that had never, in all the long months behind her, burned itself out.

As her body responded traitorously, hungrily devouring all it had ached, needed, and yearned for to an almost absurd degree, Haley realized that nothing about her addiction to this man had changed. She had managed to escape him only for a while, to avoid what surely would have consumed her, destroyed her.

As one large hand left her side to slide upward, cupping the firmness of one breast within its palm, Haley shuddered, gathering every reserve she could manage to pull away, turning her head to the side. Lance's averted lips found solace in the tender flesh of her cheek and then the sensitive spot behind her ear.

"Lance . . . please." Her voice was thick and raspy, mincing the resolve she'd hoped to muster.

His answer was a muffled groan as he continued his ruthless exploration of her neck, forcing her head to tilt backward as he located the pulse point within the delicate ivory hollow of her throat.

"Lance," she managed in a more forceful tone. "Please . . . stop."

She could feel his reluctance as he obligingly released her from the strength of his grip, his granite features revealing some inner battle that was raging within him as he struggled to conquer his runaway desire.

"Why?" he asked, a dark flame flickering within his eyes as he created a small distance between them, unwilling as yet to release her completely.

"Are you going to deny you enjoyed kissing me, Haley?" he asked, his sarcasm digging into her.

"No," she threw back at him, her amber eyes glowing like topaz, her features tightening grimly. "I'm not going to deny it. Yes, I did enjoy it, if you want to hear me say it. And yes, I would like you to make love to me. Yes, you turn me on." She paused, glaring at him. "There. Does that satisfy your ego for now?"

Lance gazed down at her shrewdly; the bluntness of her response seemed to intrigue him.

"Then why the pretended reluctance?" he asked, his stare unwavering in its demand for a forthright answer.

"I'm not pretending!" Haley retorted, her anger sparked now. She shirked roughly from his loosened hold on her and managed to step away, her hands crossing and grasping her arms above the elbows, rubbing them up and down in agitation. Lance made no move to come to her, but nevertheless she took a defensive step backward.

"Tell me one good reason why we should just fall into each other's arms the moment we're alone together?" she asked, her cheeks tinged with the heat of her emotions.

"Give me one why we shouldn't," Lance countered, crossing his arms against his chest and resting one hip on the edge of the desk that Haley had just vacated.

"You said yourself you enjoyed it." He cast her a knowing look. "Not that I had to be told."

"You know as well as I that that's not a good enough reason," Haley stated firmly. "On the other hand I suppose if you're the type of person who doesn't give a damn who gets hurt by your careless attitude toward fooling around, then simple desire is reason enough."

Lance glared at Haley for a moment, some dark emotion sweeping across the angular planes of his rugged features. When he spoke, his voice was as cold as ice, slicing straight through Haley as he responded bitterly.

"If you are referring," he said finally, "to our relationship before Julia and I were married—as no doubt you are—then may I remind you that you were very much a party to my supposed indiscretion. If anyone hadn't any qualms about 'fooling around' at the time, it was you. As I recall, it didn't take much for me to persuade you to share my bed. And yours, too," he added, a cynical smile lifting one corner of his wide mouth.

Haley's face darkened as something inside her exploded at his indelicate—though all too accurate—recounting of their affair. She had been all too eager to fall into his arms then: a ripe fruit just waiting to be plucked by his greedy hands; an easy, completely available side dish for his insatiable appetite. But he wasn't being fair. She'd never been without an almost inordinate amount of guilt over the whole sordid affair.

"You know very well, Lance Sullivan," she seethed, spitting out the words between labored breaths, "that I tried to break off our relationship. Many times! It was you who was always ready to talk me back into just one more time. What a fool I was!"

"Ah, but a quite willing one," Lance sneered, his

features contorted by the blazing look that shot across his face.

"Why, you—you bastard!" Haley sputtered, her fury spilling over, hands swiftly disengaging their protective hold across her chest to be clenched tightly at her sides.

"After all you did, after all the pain you caused, you can stand there and spew out self-righteous statements like that!" Haley's eyes blazed, and her voice waivered, but she had been provoked beyond measure now.

Lance's face had hardened into an angry mask, but Haley ignored it, fully intending to get it all out now.

"Let me make this clear," she went on, amber eyes glinting in resentment. "I'll be the first to admit that I fell into your clever trap only too willingly. I was a sorry victim of my own instincts, and to this day I haven't been able to forgive myself for it. Believe me, I was brought up with the highest morals and principles. The last thing in the world I ever intended to do was deceive my very best friend!"

Haley hesitated, aware that she was shaking from this emotional outpouring but unable to stop the flow of it. "But it happened," she raged on, "and there's nothing I can do except accept the fact that I made a mistake—blame it on my inexperience or something like that." She paused, a corner of her mouth twitching spasmodically. "But what I can't ever seem to come to terms with is the picture of utter vulnerability I must have made to you. It's one thing to seduce a girl and introduce her to a world of sensuality that she'd never even had a hint of. But to take it a step further, to have her believe that you

80

have more of an interest than merely a sexual one is—is nothing but a crime." Haley's voice broke with those last words and she swallowed, a useless attempt to ease the burning constriction at the back of her throat. God help her, but she wasn't going to break down in front of him!

"Haley, I—" Lance began, pushing himself off the desk and taking a step in her direction.

Haley held up a hand to stop him from advancing farther. "No. I'm not through." Her hands itched for some distracting motion, anything to keep her fingernails from continuing to dig painfully into the flesh of her palms. She took a few steps toward Mike's desk, picking up a silver letter opener and absently sliding her fingers up and down its shiny length.

"I think you should listen to all of this, Lance. Not that I think it will change you, of course. But perhaps it will show you how easily toying with someone's affections can cause an incredible amount of harm."

She studied the silver letter opener in her hand, her brow lined with furrows of bitter remembrance.

"I really believed you, you know. In spite of everything, all the doubts—the realizations that I would lose the best friend I ever had. I was willing to give it all up for you." The letter opener blurred, and she blinked hard, a tiny droplet trickling its way down and falling onto the silvery surface. Her thumb absently rubbed it into the cool metal. "You see," she whispered, the burning in her throat now an aching ball of pain, "I thought I was in love with you." She laughed, a small pitiful sound. "What a joke," she muttered. "Really funny, isn't it?" Suddenly the letter opener slid from her fingers and clattered onto the parquet floor. Haley's shoulders slumped and she lifted one hand, fingers pressing in on either side of the bridge of her nose.

She wept silently, her shoulders heaving, her breathing ragged and sparse. She had tried, she had really tried, to get this all out in a reasonable manner. But she'd held it inside too long, letting it fester to enormous proportions. Why hadn't she had the common sense to get this all out of her system before now? The last thing her pride needed was to allow Lance to glimpse her vulnerablity, to know how much she'd been hurt.

But she'd done just that, exposing everything. . . . Blinded by her tears, unable to stop their relentless flow, she felt herself being pulled into a circle of warmth, a pair of firm, sinewy arms wrapping themselves around her back, drawing her close against the wall of hard flat torso that felt so familiar, so natural, as it pressed against her breasts.

A hand was stroking the soft sheen of her golden auburn hair, and after a while the outpouring was stemmed. Haley could feel the tear-soaked dampness of Lance's sweater, could hear her breathing coming now in spasmodic spurts between bouts of sniffling.

Lance released one of his arms, wrapping the other about her shoulders and leading her alongside him to the leather love seat that stood against one wall. On the way he snatched several tissues from the box that stood on Haley's temporary desk, then sat her down on the soft couch, his heavier weight creating an incline that caused her body to slant toward his.

Haley sat stiffly forward, her hands damp from wiping the wetness from her cheeks and beneath her eyes. She accepted the tissues from Lance and unceremoniously began to blow her nose.

"Enough?" Lance asked. "Do you need any more?"

Haley shook her head and finally regained enough control to lift her reddened puffy eyes to his. His expression had softened considerably, and she met his gaze now evenly.

"I apologize," Haley said softly. "I really hadn't intended on making such a scene, believe me."

"You needn't make apologies for saying what you really feel," Lance said quietly. "I'm glad you got it all out. Are you willing, though, to listen to my side of the story?"

Haley stared at the neckline of his sweater and chewed on her lower lip, as if trying to discern the intricate pattern of the knitted blue-and-green threads. She wondered how he could possibly add to what she'd accused him of, other than merely admitting his guilt, but she lifted a shoulder as she answered softly. "Go ahead."

Lance uttered a gruff laugh, though the gray-green eyes held not an ounce of humor. "What I have to say may not make any impression on you whatsoever. I suppose my actions back then made me into an ogre of the worst sort. I can't blame you for hating me." He looked away then, his voice dropping to a somber note as he added, "There've been times when I've hated myself for the unutterable mess I allowed my life to become." He glanced back at Haley, who was studying the play of emotion across the normally stoic face.

"I'm sure you'll find it hard to believe, Haley, but

my intentions at the time were honorable. I never intended for you to get hurt the way you did."

Haley stared mutely at him for a moment, wanting to believe him, something inside her even hoping there was a grain of truth in what he was saying. She cast him a skeptical look.

"You found it easy enough to ignore the fact that I might get hurt when you led me on the way you did, Lance. But . . . you know, I've had a lot of time to think about what happened. No matter what you did, no matter whom you chose, someone had to get hurt. Considering Julia's reaction to your divorcing her, I can see now that my pain was far less than hers would have been."

Lance narrowed his eyes as if suddenly blinded by some stark light. "Julia." He breathed the word. "There's no way to avoid *that* subject, I suppose."

Haley stared at Lance with disbelieving eyes. Never had she seen or heard such venomous regard for another person from anyone—least of all Lance, who had heretofore portrayed an uncaring, totally uninterested attitude toward his former wife.

"Lance, how can you talk about her that way? She was your wife for over two years! She loved you more than anything! She even suffered a nervous break-down because of you."

Lance's head swung back around, and the disdain-ful expression it bore stunned Haley.

"You haven't changed at all, have you? You're still the same naive girl you were back then. I thought you said you learned a lot while you were gone."

84

The biting sarcasm in Lance's tone went straight through her, and she was at a loss for a response.

"I—I don't know why you're talking to me like this," she said at last. "But I can see that *you've* changed. I don't remember you ever sounding so—so hateful and bitter."

"No, I don't suppose you would." Lance bit out the words. "But then, as you say, I have changed. I've become a hardened man, as they say in all the books."

Haley frowned at what seemed a completely different man sitting next to her. He had brought up one leg, resting the ankle atop the knee of the other, and, preoccupied and tense, he plucked at the fabric stretched across it. There was something behind all this carefully controlled anger he was exhibiting, and she temporarily forgot her own tumultous emotions of only a few minutes earlier. She'd never seen Lance so intense, so burdened with whatever it was he had obviously been carrying inside all this time. Was she going to hold on to her own anger and resentment as if she was the only one hurt by their ill-fated affair? Something deep within told her she'd be a fool not to listen to him now. Gently she touched the sleeve of his sweater, her tone soft and quiet as she spoke.

"Lance . . . what are you talking about? I don't understand—really."

Slowly his gaze lifted to meet hers, the coldness in the pale green depths softening as he said, "No, you really don't, do you?" He hesitated, as if mulling something over in his mind, then continued.

"You're so attached to that juvenile image you have of yourself and Julia as lifetime pals that you'll never be able to face the truth of the matter until someone throws it in your face."

Haley frowned in confusion, but she said nothing, waiting for Lance to continue in this strange vein.

"I hate to be the one to tell you all this, Haley . . . I can see that you really have been living in a dream world all this time." He paused deliberately. "Julia Morris is not now, nor has she been in a very long time, one of your friends. To say nothing of being your so-called 'best' friend."

There was no malice in Lance's voice or expression as he spoke, but the words were like a slap in Haley's face.

"You don't know that," she shot back indignantly. "Julia and I—"

"I know," Lance interrupted. "You've been the best of friends since you were children. You don't have to continue. I know it all by heart."

Haley opened her mouth to interrupt, but Lance cut her off. "I'm not saying any of this to be cruel, Haley, believe me. But you must remember, I lived with the woman for over two years, and what I came to learn surpasses any sort of knowledge about her you may have thought you had."

Haley sat dumbstruck, amazed at what she was hearing. Some masochistic impulse in her, though, wanted to hear more of it, no matter how painful it might be.

"Julia is a very troubled woman, Haley. As much as it may have surprised you, her nervous breakdown came as a surprise to none of her family—least of all to me. She is a conniving, self-centered person who'll do anything to get what she wants. I was idiot enough to get roped into marrying her, and stupider for sticking around when I should have kicked her out the moment I learned how she had deceived me."

Haley frowned in consternation, not believing what she was hearing.

"What do you mean—she deceived you?" she asked, eyes widening as she awaited his reply.

"It's quite a story," Lance said dryly. "After I had finally convinced you that I was going to break my engagement with Julia, to tell her that I wanted my freedom"—Lance cast Haley a direct look—" I did just that. I broke it to her as easily as I could, but she reacted like some—some wild thing. I'd never seen anything like it. She accused me of having slept with you. . . ." Seeing Haley's thunderstruck face, her mouth parting in an astonished gape, Lance nodded. "Yes. She did." He continued soberly. "She never trusted you, Haley. Never. She told me that often enough. Especially how she'd always known you'd thought you were better than her. Smarter." At the pained expression on Haley's face, Lance uttered a short, gruff sound. "God knows, she was right about that." His gaze focused on Haley's hurt one. "She was jealous of you, Haley. Unbearably jealous."

Haley studied the floor for a moment, struggling to absorb all this, almost overwhelmed by it. Finally she lifted her head. "But how—" she began, the bridge of her nose lined with a deep vertical crease.

"I don't know how she found out about us," Lance continued. "I don't believe she really knew it for a fact. She was simply grasping at anything, at anyone on whom to place the blame. She couldn't face the fact that my wanting to break it off had nothing to

87

do with wanting anyone else. We were simply wrong for each other."

Lance drew in a deep breath, then went on. "However, I didn't deny the accusation. I admitted that we'd been seeing each other, that I'd been attracted to you ever since I'd met you."

With that Haley slumped back into the couch, every ounce of hope and resolve draining out of her as her mind reeled with the import of what Lance was revealing. Julia had known; all this time she had known about her and Lance's supposedly "discreet" affair.

That simple piece of information touched on so many things; it tainted everything that had happened after the day Julia had so happily informed Haley that she and Lance were moving up their wedding date. Even when Haley had visited Julia in the hospital she had known. . . . Haley brought both hands up to cup over her eyes, her fingers massaging the steadily increasing throb in her temples. It was too much—too much to comprehend.

Lance went on. "My admission, however, made no difference. She said she didn't care how many women I had slept with, she would not let me shirk my responsibilities, not let me leave her alone with an illegimate child."

Haley's head snapped up in shock, amazed at this new twist in an already unbelievable story.

"That, of course, threw me off—as it was intended to. I knew it was possible—" Lance broke off, noticing the questioning hurt in Haley's eyes.

"I had not slept with her since I met you, Haley. Whatever ideas you may have developed about my

88

moral character, you'll simply have to take my word that I find it distasteful to bed two women simultaneously."

Haley stared mutely, waiting for him to go on.

"She claimed to be in her third month. When I asked her why she hadn't told me before then, she said she hadn't known for sure until a few days previously. She had me there." Lance paused, then lifted one shoulder slightly as he said quietly, "I think you know the rest."

Haley was unable to speak for several minutes, the weight of Lance's revelation beginning to soak through her reluctant mind. It seemed too incredible to believe: that Julia had known all along that she and Lance had had an affair; that Julia had been pregnant with his child all that time. How terribly hurt she must have been. Haley cringed with the understanding of what such a predicament could do to a woman.

"How horrible for her," Haley said. "I would have never guessed she was suffering so much."

"Don't get your sympathies all worked up," Lance commented dispassionately.

Haley's expression was one of consternation. "What is that supposed to mean? Even to think of the poor thing being pregnant all that time and—"

"She wasn't," Lance interrupted bluntly.

"What?" Haley blinked in confusion.

"She wasn't pregnant," Lance stated flatly. "It was a lie. A carefully thought out and played out lie to convince me to marry her."

Haley sat in stunned silence, everything Lance was telling her seeming like some plot to a soap opera.

Surely he couldn't be sitting here saying all this. Surely she was dreaming.

"Of course, it worked, just as she had planned. I married her out of obligation to my unborn child." Lance cast Haley a meaningful glance. "And for no other reason than that." He paused, then went on. "She fooled me completely. Shortly after you left, she feigned a miscarriage." Slowly he shook his head, as if the memory of it all still haunted him. "It was a superb act, deserving of an Oscar. I really felt sorry for Julia then. There was no way I could leave her. Aside from my own sympathies I would have been the town monster—which, at the time," he added dryly, "I could little afford. I was just taking over for Dad, and I had enough problems moving into the position without inviting more."

"How did you find out—" Haley began.

"How did I find out that she never was pregnant in the first place? Quite innocently, as a matter of fact. We were at a party at the Ladwigs'. Michael Ladwig was her gynecologist, and I asked him if he thought Julia would always have trouble carrying full-term. He asked me what I meant, and after I brought up her miscarriage, his reaction was enough. He told me that Julia, to his knowledge, had never been pregnant. She'd claimed he was her doctor at the time; I was too busy to do anything at the time other than accept her word at face value."

Lance shifted, uncrossing his legs and stretching them out before him. He let out a long breath, then went on. "It was then that I realized what an idiot she must have taken me for. Shortly after, I told her

90

I wanted a divorce. It was the same scene all over again. Only this time a little more dramatic."

"What do you mean?" Haley asked, intrigued.

"She overdosed on some sleeping medication." Haley's eyes widened, and she gasped in disbelief.

Lance waved a dismissing hand. "Oh, that, too, was one of her carefully thought out ruses. She didn't take enough to do anything more than sleep a long time, but it sure as hell scared everyone. Anyway her parents begged me to give it another year, to see if there was absolutely no way we could work things out.

"I knew it was hopeless, of course, but I had then —and I still do—a great deal of respect for the Morrises. My work kept me busy enough, so that I never had to face the fact that we still lived and ate in the same house." Lance slid Haley a rueful glance. "Sleeping was a different matter.

"However, I was gone most of the time, so that made no real difference either."

Suddenly there was a noise downstairs, the sound of the heavy front door being opened and footsteps walking across the stone entryway, hushing as they fell across the plush carpeting of the main hallway.

Lance stood, walking toward the window and twisting the Plexiglas rod to open the miniblinds.

"Must be Mike," he said, looking down on the parking lot below. As if in confirmation, Mike's booming greeting drifted up the staircase he was ascending.

Haley rose rapidly from the couch, running her fingers through her hair and rubbing a thumb beneath each eye, to wipe away any telltale mascara

91

smears. She walked around to the back of her desk, and was just sitting down in her chair as Mike walked in.

CHAPTER SIX

"Well, look who's here," Mike greeted them both jovially, walking into the room and leaving the door open behind him. "I noticed the car in the lot as I was passing by, and decided to check things out."

"Hello, Mike," Lance greeted his manager.

"Lance, glad to see you," Mike said, accepting the older man's hand and shaking it briskly. "Hello, Haley. Working on Sunday. How commendable."

Haley greeted him and smiled, then Lance commented, "Since I'm not paying Miss Jordenson for a ski vacation, I demanded that she show me what she's going to be spending my hard-earned money on."

"Good idea." Mike nodded his approval, smiling. "When did you get in? I didn't expect you until the middle of the week."

"I wrapped up everything back in Littleton sooner than I'd expected to, and my travel agent was able to book me on a flight yesterday, so I took it."

"Great," Mike enthused. "I have quite a lot to discuss with you anyway. We can use the extra time."

"Where are you headed?" Haley asked, taking in the tight-fitting black ski pants and short black-and-beige parka he was wearing. "It's obvious you didn't drop in for a little overtime."

"No way," Mike confirmed, waving a hand toward the bright sunlight filtering through the window. "Not with this kind of a day. I'm headed for Mount Norquay."

"Is it opened yet?" Lance sounded surprised.

"Not all of it. But enough for me to get in a day's worth of the fresh powder dumped last night."

"I take it you've been taking advantage of everything Banff has to offer."

"You bet," Mike confirmed. "It's been a terrific season so far. Promises to get even better. You're going to get in a few runs yourself, I assume?"

"Naturally," Lance agreed. "But not until I see how things have been coming along here."

"So far, so good," Mike said. "There is one problem I could use your advice on, however. Concerns one of our kitchen suppliers."

"Let's have a look at it," Lance said briskly.

"All right."

Lance started to follow Mike out of the room, then stopped, turning around to face Haley.

"Are you going to stay up here?" he asked, the pale green eyes filled with a soft light of concern.

"I think so," Haley answered. "I have a few things to go over. It's okay," she added, the double meaning in her words obvious to Lance.

Lance nodded and followed Mike downstairs. Haley listened to the clatter of their boots resounding on the stairway as they descended into the lower level of the restaurant. She had been holding a pen in one hand in pretense of really doing something, but it dropped from her fingers now, rolling across the edge of the desk and dropping silently onto the floor. Haley paid it no heed, however, as she stood and moved across the room to stand by the window;

94

once there, she seemed to have no recollection of her legs moving her to that position. *How very strange,* she thought; *even the sunlight seems different to me now.* It was as though, having had her eyes opened to the truth of what had really occurred during that painful period of her life two and a half years ago, she had been awakened from some hazy, confusing dream.

Everything Lance had just revealed had changed her life—in one short hour. It was incredible, wasn't it? It was like some stark, painful glare that cast the very world she was looking upon now into startling relief; as if an abstract painting she had been studying but whose meaning she had never actually grasped had been transformed into a canvas of realism, a simple portrait of the way her life had really been all this time.

Sadly she shook her head, the sunlight adding a red-gold sheen to her auburn tresses. Had she really been that naïve, that blind to what her real relationship with Julia had been all that time? If what Lance had revealed was indeed true—and she knew deep down that the story was too incredible for him to have made up—then she really had been a ridiculously naive young woman at the time, too ignorant to see the obvious hate and resentment Julia must have felt toward her.

Why hadn't Julia confronted her with the knowledge of her affair with Lance? They could have had it out then and there. Haley knew that if it had been she, she would have done just that. She would have ranted and raved and screamed, but it would have all come out, regardless of what would have happened to her relationship with Julia. And who knew? Perhaps it would have even had a chance of surviving anyway.

But Julia had held it all in; she had swallowed her pride where Lance was concerned and tricked him into marrying her. Why would she do such a thing? Marry a man who said he didn't love her, who admitted that he had been seeing her best friend?

The answer came to Haley so suddenly, so sharply, it was as though a searing knife had penetrated the very core of her being. Julia had gone through with the marriage to get back at her. Revenge—pure and simple revenge—had turned her into a conniving, scheming woman, a woman who would do anything to hurt Haley as badly as she had been hurt.

Haley suddenly recalled how Julia had told her the news that she and Lance were moving the wedding date up. Haley had done her best to hide her shock, to pretend that she was happy for Julia. Now, of course, she knew how Julia must have seen through her act—and how delighted she must have felt at Haley's discomfort.

Lance was totally correct about one thing, Haley thought, wincing at the silent admission. Julia was a consummate actress, her deliberate pretense of continued friendship deserving of an Oscar. Right up to the very end, when Haley had left Littleton for Philadelphia, she had carried on about how much she was going to miss Haley, that she would correspond and call. Of course, she had done neither, and after a few obligatory letters on Haley's part—with no response —she herself had discontinued the communication, believing that Julia was too busy with her new marriage to have the time to communicate with her.

Haley felt sick at the remembrance of Julia's innocent statement a few weeks ago that she had always thought Lance would have been happier with someone like Haley. Haley would never have guessed that she had been taunting her, playing with her emotions.

The thought suddenly struck her that perhaps Julia had been acting even in the hospital. That seemed to be the only thing the woman was capable of doing. Was she that desperate for attention that she would resort to staging a nervous breakdown? Before today Haley would have scoffed at any such judgment, but now . . . now it seemed all the more plausible.

And what about Lance's part in all this? Ah, Haley thought wearily, that was another matter entirely, one she wasn't sure she could cope with at the moment. Her mind was boggled with the incredible revelations she'd been exposed to today. She honestly didn't think she could bear the thought of any more.

So absorbed had she become in her own somber reverie that the heavy footsteps approaching from behind startled her, causing her to jump as she pivoted around to face Lance.

"Sorry," he said. "I didn't mean to scare you."

"It's all right." Haley shrugged the apology aside, and walked back to her desk.

"Are you all right?" Lance asked quietly, a note of concern in his voice.

"Yes. I'm fine," Haley answered. "Where's Mike?"

"That's what I came back up to talk to you about. He's been trying his best to convince me not to waste this gorgeous day and to go along with him for some skiing."

Haley nodded, not moving from her position behind the desk, Lance's words not really registering.

"Would you like to go? Mount Norquay is certainly not the easiest skiing around these parts, but I'm sure you could handle it." He grinned and raised his eyebrows. "How 'bout it?"

"I— Thanks anyway, Lance, but I don't think so. I'm really not in the mood."

Lance walked around the desk and stood beside her, placing one hand on her forearm.

"Haley, I didn't mean to upset you. I realize what I told you has been a hell of a shock. But the best thing you could do would be forget about it—at least for now. Believe me, it's not worth the headache."

Haley pursed her lips and sighed heavily. "You're right. What you've told me has shocked me—just as you warned me. . . . I'll get used to it though. I just want to have some time alone, that's all." She paused, managing a tiny smile as she gazed up at him.

"You go on with Mike. Have a good time. But I'd really like to stay here awhile longer. Do you think you could both take Mike's car and leave me yours? That way I would have a way back to the hotel. Mike could drop you off when you return."

Lance gave a brief nod. "Of course. Are you sure you'll be all right?"

Haley chuckled softly. "Of course. I'm not a basket case. And besides, I've plenty to do before leaving for Calgary tomorrow. I may as well get it finished today. That way I can leave directly from the hotel in the morning and get back earlier."

"Okay," Lance said. "I'd better get going then. We've already lost an hour and a half of lift time." He turned and headed for the door.

"Have a good time," Haley called out after him.

"I will." Lance smiled back at her. "See you later."

Haley watched his retreating figure, the pleasure that lean, rugged body had once evoked from hers suddenly assaulting her memory in almost painful waves. Inwardly she was a quivering mass; the knowledge of how she had once responded to the gentle coaxing of his skilled manliness filled her even now with a wanting—an aching so exquisite, it made all the other emotions she had suffered today pale by comparison.

The sound of Mike's car roaring to life outside brought her back to reality, and her gaze focused on the catalog she was holding in her hands, though she couldn't remember how it had got there. If she were to make good her intention of getting the preliminaries for tomorrow's task out of the way, then she'd better get started.

It was three o'clock in the afternoon before Haley decided to wrap up for the day. She drove back to the hotel slowly, willing herself to think about nothing but the picturesque little town she had come to consider one of the quaintest she had ever seen.

Driving into town from the north, she followed the town's main street, Banff Avenue, giving close attention to the conglomeration of hotels, restaurants, stores, and nightspots that lined the broad, bustling thoroughfare, thinking how it all resembled an alpine village. She would simply *have* to get in a little shopping while she was here. She would never forgive herself—nor would her mother, come to think of it—if she passed up the opportunity to purchase a few memorable items.

By the time she had reached the Banff Springs, parked the car, and made her way through the enormous structure up to her room, Haley realized that she had actually been successful in putting her earlier preoccupation with Lance's pronouncements concerning Julia out of her mind for a longer amount of time than she would have imagined possible.

Good! Some staunch, inner voice was making itself heard by now, asserting that she'd do well to put the matter out of her mind for the rest of her stay here. What good could come of brooding over the matter anyway? She was here for a purpose, and she was not going to let anything get in the way of accomplishing it. *Forget about Julia!* Haley admonished herself. *There'll be time enough to come to terms with her, and it's wasteful to use your time thinking about her.*

Haley's resolution was logical and practical and should have been carried out, but unfortunately, she discovered, arriving at it was a good deal easier than putting it into practice. Every time she would successfully get her mind on other matters, thoughts of Julia and Lance, and herself, the strange way in which their lives had intermingled, bringing pain to all three of them, kept invading, destroying her concentration.

She was hungry, but she hadn't the least desire to leave her room and go downstairs for supper. Instead, she phoned room service, but when the meal arrived, she merely picked at the food, her appetite almost nonexistent.

Lance's call that evening was just the thing she needed. By then she had had more than enough of her own company, filled with nothing but brooding reflections, and she accepted quite readily his invitation to join him in one of the pubs for a drink. She dressed with pleasure, happy to get out of the jeans and sweater she had worn all day long. She slipped into a cream silk blouse, tucking the soft material beneath the waistband of a pair of dark brown velvet slacks. After making use of her curling iron, she brushed out her hair, the soft auburn waves framing her porcelain face in a flowing style that beckoned roaming, desirous male hands. Unwilling to analyze her motives for the pains she was taking with her appearance, Haley slipped into a pair of ankle-strapped beige shoes and pulled on a matching velvet blazer. Dropping the room key into the pocket, she left.

The hotel was buzzing tonight, Haley discovered as she crossed the enormous stone-floored lobby, noticing that virtually every piece of velvet-covered Victorian-style furniture was occupied, the palatial hall filled with sounds of merriment. Tonight one of the hotel's four restaurants was hosting, as it did on a weekly basis, a medieval banquet, complete with authentically dressed lords and ladies, court jesters, and sexily clad maidens prepared to serve in the

101

manner of the days of knighthood: it would be an evening of guaranteed feasting and revelry.

Haley walked slowly through the throng of people awaiting admission, her head moving from side to side as she took in the wondrous loveliness of it all.

Six beautifully decorated twenty-five-foot Christmas trees winked and glimmered the entire lengths of their heavily laden boughs. The sounds of a live band somewhere blended in with the other festive noises. A sudden sense of excitement gripped Haley; the Christmas season always brought the promise of joy and merriment, which now permeated every fiber of her being. No wonder her sister, Greta, had gushed so about this place. It was in every way the perfect place for a holiday.

"Did you get lost?" The deep voice behind her was startling, but Haley turned and faced Lance with a smile on her face.

"No," she answered lightly. "Am I late?"

Lance shook his head of curling tawny locks, his pale green eyes deliberately, openly raking the length of her.

"You look ravishing tonight," he said huskily.

"Thank you," Haley replied, color rising to tinge her cheeks with a melon glow. She thought she could have easily told him the same. The sheer male magnetism of his tall granite-hard physique lent a superbly distinguished appeal to the casual clothes he had worn tonight.

Black tweed slacks molded themselves along the long tight runner's hips and thighs, his turtleneck gray and white sweater defining the broadness of chest and shoulders, the flat trim abdomen.

Haley felt a lurch in her chest as Lance casually, almost proprietarily took her arm, leading her out of the crowded room toward a wide red-carpeted stairway at the farther end, which lead to a second, partially exposed level.

"I thought this would be more acceptable," he said, leading her through the door of the dark-paneled dimly lighted pub, the sounds of the rest of the hotel dissipating as they found a secluded corner table.

"It's perfect," Haley commented, taking her seat as Lance rolled the leather-upholstered chair out for her.

The cocktail waitress arrived promptly and took their orders for drinks. Lance leaned back in his chair afterward, smiling curiously at the look Haley was giving him.

"What are you staring at?" he asked bemusedly.

"Your nose," Haley replied, an amused grin lighting her delicate features as she bent forward to study it better.

Lance automatically reached up and ran one finger up and down the subject of Haley's scrutiny.

"What's wrong with it? Did it grow an inch or two?"

Haley laughed softly. "Silly. No, it's just that it really looks different—all red and shiny—sort of like Rudolph's, you know."

"All right," Lance said dryly, cocking an eyebrow. "I'll let you get away with that. For now."

Haley ignored the gibe, commenting, "There must have been lots of sunshine where you skied today."

"There was," Lance confirmed. "We had perfect

103

weather all day. Most of the slopes were open, and we didn't stop until the last lift closed." He hesitated, concern peeking through the mask of roughly carved features.

"How was your day?" he asked quietly, his real interest not escaping Haley's assessment of the question.

"Fine," she answered. "I got a lot done." She knew he was seeking another reply, one more indicative of her reaction to their discussion earlier this morning, but she was reluctant to bring the subject up. She had finally managed to shove it aside mentally, and the evening was too charming to rehash the matter now.

"I narrowed down my choices of what I'm going to be looking for at the publisher's house in Calgary tomorrow."

Lance gave a slight nod, indicating his interest, yet hinting at his understanding of her need to pursue other topics for the moment. "I'd like to hear about them," he said, adding, "We never did get around to that subject this morning."

With that Haley took off into a full-scale discussion of what she thought most appropriate for Lance's new restaurant. Lance listened quietly as Haley went on about her plans to obtain original graphics from the publisher's house in Calgary: she was considering a mixture of abstracts in various media—relief printings, etchings, lithographs, anything she thought would blend in with her other acquisitions, which would be the more interesting aspect of her search.

She had in mind to visit local galleries, in hopes of

obtaining paintings and perhaps a few statuary items indicative of western Canada, with emphasis on the country's vast, regal mountains and abundant free-roaming wildlife.

Haley was obviously in her element, her expression and voice revealing only too clearly her immense pleasure in what she was doing. Lance was attentive, injecting a question now and then, feeding Haley's enthusiastic exposition. Totally unaware of the portrait of loveliness she made, her enlived features bathed in the warm candlelight's glow, she gave no notice to the stirrings she was creating within Lance, evidenced by a certain darkening of the cool, pale green irises.

The evening progressed in continued amicability. Finally, having exhausted the subject of her own work, Haley politely steered the conversation to draw out Lance. He slipped easily into a discussion of the restaurant business, an endeavor he'd thought would never be able to maintain his interest, but which he had discovered to be surprisingly fulfilling.

Only an unsuccessfully stifled yawn on Haley's part reminded them both of the lateness of the hour. Lance took care of the check and escorted Haley back outside, sounds of revelry and music coming in muted tones from another part of the vast hotel complex.

As they walked through the magical surroundings —the stuff of fairy tales and happily-ever-afters—so reminicent of medieval days, Haley slipped easily into the protective snugness of Lance's arm around her shoulders. It felt so right, being here beside the man she had anguished over all these years. Somehow it was just as she'd remembered it, yet different. So very different. Was this the same man she had so rigorously trained herself to forget, to assign to the past as a heartbreaking, regrettable mistake?

They were the only passengers on the slow-moving elevator besides the ever present operator, but Lance drew Haley up close beside him in one corner, his hand sliding up and down the length of her arm in tender, sensuous strokes.

As they reached the enclave just outside Haley's door Lance stopped, turning her around to face him as his arms wrapped around her lower back, tiny fingers of desire probing expectantly within her as she awaited his kiss. Lance, however, merely tilted his silhouetted features downward to gaze at her, his slightly narrowed eyes revealing some inner war.

"Haley, I—" he began, as if weighing carefully his next words.

"Shhh," Haley whispered, bringing a hand up and placing a finger over the lips she knew would possess hers momentarily. "Please. Don't say anything more." She gazed up at him, amber eyes shimmering mirrors of gold. "Lance, it wouldn't be right. . . . We can't just take up where we left off. It would be impossible. We both know that, so let's not even try it."

Staring at her for a long moment, he tightened his hold and he drew her even closer to the virile potency that seemed to be at desperate odds with what she was asking of him.

Finally he nodded his assent, lowering his head to press his feverish lips against hers, their fierce demand obviously intentional, an intensely effective imprinting of his mere temporary acceptance of her wish. Haley acquiesced to the heat of the passion that drew her to him, funneling up her heightened responses like some swirling, sweeping tornado, whisking up her better intentions in the rushing wind of her runaway senses.

Pulling herself away from the powerful grip he held her in was an exercise in utmost control. To have remained any longer under the spell of his will-dissolving kiss would have been playing with fire. Determinedly she removed her hands from his nape, not remembering how or when they had arrived in that position, placing them on the arms that surrounded her. She spoke, her voice wavering, yet somehow steady in its import.

"Lance . . . thank you for the evening. And for everything else."

With obvious reluctance Lance released her. "What time are you leaving tomorrow?" he asked, clearing his throat.

"Hopefully around eight. I'll phone you when I get back."

Lance nodded, and Haley removed the key from her pocket, slid it inside the lock, and turned it.

"Good night," Lance said, as she stepped inside the room.

"Good night," Haley returned, her voice barely above a whisper as she watched his retreating, soundless form disappear down the dimly lighted corridor.

CHAPTER SEVEN

Driving the long scenic stretch of highway toward Calgary the next morning, Haley found herself hard put to concentrate on her surroundings, however distracting they might have been. Her thoughts kept pulling Haley to the overwhelming question now facing her: What should she do about her relationship with Lance?

In spite of her assertion the night before that they could not possibly pick up where they had left off, in spite of everything Lance had revealed, Haley knew deep within her heart there was more brawn than conviction in the statement. All the passion, all the emotional pull she had once shared with Lance had not dissipated in the years they'd been apart. If anything, her feelings had only been strengthened by the knowledge of all he had endured; her affections had been heightened by an undeniable respect and admiration for his obvious sense of moral responsibility.

Haley knew she would have been no more than a fool to try and convince herself that she was not more deeply in love with him than ever before. Yet, it was not an easy thing for one's pride to withstand, knowing that the love so painfully felt for another was unrequited.

Haley had no reservations that Lance possessed a certain affection for her, mingled with the strong element of sexual attraction he so obviously still felt. In light of everything that had happened to him—

and she had absolutely no doubt of his word at this point—she could fully understand any barriers he might have erected preventing any sort of emotional involvement with anyone.

But could she afford to let herself in for more of the well-remembered anguish that inevitably went hand and hand with what purported to be another one-sided love affair? For she had no assurance that that wasn't exactly what she was headed for once again. Lance never spoke of it, yet Haley suspected strongly that he was just as much involved with his restaurant business as he'd always been. His relationship with Julia would certainly have driven any man to the extremes he'd gone to to be away from her, but somehow Haley sensed there was more to his intense involvement in his work. He needed it, just as his father had needed it; it was in his blood. She doubted seriously he'd give that up for any woman. She couldn't resent this about him, of course; with her new business she was caught up in the same web herself, wasn't she?

Well, it was all pretty much academic at this point anyway. Now she was in control of the situation, and she would hang on to that like a lifeline. She had let herself be caught up by the passionate instinct that was a chemical reaction between the two of them, but surely that was within her control. She had no intention of losing Lance as a friend or a business associate —that was too valuable a relationship to forsake. But she could—she *would*—redirect the relationship to exclude anything more than that.

Buoyed by the positive element of her decision, Haley realized that this was a more significant turning point in her life than her leaving Littleton two and a half years ago. She would really be putting the past behind her now—a love that was never meant to be and a friend she had never really had. Whereas she had merely run from the problem before, she was now facing it squarely. She swelled inwardly with the knowledge that she was capable of taking her life in her own hands and moving forward.

Having come to a more definite state of mind as to where she was headed, Haley was able to face the rest of the day with a great deal more clarity of purpose. She spent a busy nonstop day at the publisher's, selecting and purchasing the artwork she finally decided was appropriate for the restaurant. She was pleased to find a wonderful piece of statuary that she thought would be ideal as a focal point for the restaurant's spacious cocktail lounge. Unfortunately the piece had been sold, and a duplicate would have to be placed on order from the publisher's subsidiary house in San Francisco. It was the only unsatisfying part of Haley's day, but she managed to convince the agent that its undelayed procurement was absolutely imperative.

Satisfied that she had been able to make most of the purchases she had set out for, Haley left Calgary by four o'clock that afternoon, not nearly as tired as she would have thought after such a long, involved day.

Upon arrival at her room, she discovered a note from Lance, slipped beneath her door, requesting that she join him and Mike for supper if she felt up to it when she returned. A step in the right direction, Haley mused, thankful that Lance had thought to include Mike, a gesture that clearly demonstrated his respect for her desire to keep their relationship on a subdued level.

The businesslike tone in Lance's note was even more reassuring, and Haley immediately set about taking a hot bath and dressing in order to meet the two of them at the specified time.

The evening lived up to Haley's hopes, turning out to be a useful meeting for the three of them, who, from now until the restaurant's opening, would have their work cut out for them. Lance put Haley at ease with his more formal demeanor toward her, politely discussing her acquisitions in Calgary and questioning her about her scheduled visits to local galleries. Afterward Haley left for her room alone; Lance made no offer to accompany her.

The remainder of the week continued with Lance and Haley both barely having time to hold more than a few minutes worth of conversation. Haley was pleased with the way things were working out now. She felt more comfortable with Lance than she had in a very long time, and her visits to the local galleries proved to be interesting as well as fruitful.

Everything was running so smoothly that Haley was quite unprepared for the snag that marred her heretofore well-executed plans. She had placed a call to the publishing house in Calgary to check on the statuary that had been ordered from San Francisco. With an acute sense of disappointment she listened as the agent informed her the shipment wouldn't arrive until the week after Christmas, a mere few

111

days before the intended restaurant opening on New Year's Eve.

Haley felt a tremendous letdown. She had set her hopes on seeing to the completed installment of the entire selection of artwork by the middle of next week. That would have given her time to fly back home to be with her parents for Christmas. She hated to leave even one piece in anyone else's hands. Perturbed, she decided to discuss the matter with Lance immediately.

As if on cue Lance walked into the office where she was sitting behind her desk, one hand on the receiver she had just replaced in its cradle.

"What's that look for?" he asked, slanting Haley a curious glance as he crossed the room to the file cabinet next to Mike's desk.

"You're just the person I need to see," Haley said, unable to supress the baleful tone in her voice.

"Is it that bad?" Lance asked, his tawny features assuming a slightly bemused expression.

"I suppose it depends on how you look at it," Haley began, slumping back in her chair, a worried frown creasing her normally smooth brow. She immediately launched into a full disclosure of the problem concerning the artwork, a piece she was absolutely dependent on to pull together the decor she had in mind for the cocktail lounge.

Lance seemed to mull over what she had just related, then said, "I'm sure we could take care of it if that's all that remains to be installed. However, seeing as how you want to oversee the entire operation" —he nodded in deference to her obvious sense of dedication—"why don't you stay? You've already come this far anyway, you may as well see what Christmas is like in these parts."

Haley's mouth slackened slightly at the suggestion. "Oh, but I can't do that. . . ."

"Why not?" Lance lifted one shoulder expressively. "What do you have waiting back in Littleton? Another job lined up already?"

"No, of course not. Not that I know of, that is." Haley pursed her lips together, then continued. "I was planning on spending the holidays with my parents."

"Would they be terribly upset if you stayed?" Lance asked, finding what he'd been searching for in the file cabinet and closing it, then turning back to face her squarely.

Quite taken aback by the unexpectedness of Lance's suggestion, Haley had to think for a moment. "Well . . . it's not as if they'll be alone. My sister and her husband and their children will be there. I—I suppose they'd understand, since it involves my work."

"Then do it," Lance stated flatly. "That way you can be here for the grand opening on New Year's Eve."

Haley silently admitted that the idea of spending the holidays there was becoming increasingly inviting. She seemed to be absorbing the very atmosphere of the season. Being around such a friendly group of people adequately compensated for the homey surroundings she normally shared at this particular time of the year. It might be interesting to spend at least one season enjoying something other than the ordi-

113

nary. And besides, she'd have plenty to discuss when she returned home.

"You know," Haley started, smiling as she warmed to the idea of it all, "I think I'll give Mom and Dad a call. If Dad sounds to be doing all right, then I'll stay. In a way I'd hate to have done all this work and then not be able to see the reaction it's going to receive."

Lance's expression seemed to belie the dispassionate nod of his head that served as his only answer. Folder in hand, he left the room, saying he would be downstairs with Mike if she needed him for anything.

Haley stared at the telephone for a moment, hesitating a mere second before snatching it up and placing a call to her parents.

"Honey, don't you worry," her mother said after hearing her daughter's predicament. "Your father is doing just fine. Of course, we'll surely miss your not being here, but we're even happier that things have turned out so well for you up there."

Elated with her mother's enthusiastic response, Haley said, "I'll bring you both Christmas presents from here, Mom. I haven't gone shopping yet, but I'm itching to give it a whirl. The town here is everything Greta described it as—you and Dad would love it here."

"Now, don't bother yourself about silly presents if you don't have the time. Your father and I don't need anything anyway."

"I'll find something," Haley insisted. "Well, I guess I'll see you both next year. Give my love to Dad and Greta and all the others."

"All right, dear. Have a good time. Why don't you give us a call on Christmas Day, when your sister is over, and we'll all say hello."

"Good idea, Mom. Speak to you then. Take care."

Installment of the artwork Haley had chosen was to be taken care of the following Monday. It promised to be a two-day job, one which would consume almost every spare minute of her time, but meanwhile the weekend loomed ahead with virtually nothing to do. Thanks to her own efficiency she had left nothing pending, nothing with which to while away her time.

Therefore her acceptance of Lance's invitation to join him for a ski outing on Saturday was almost automatic. He suggested Sunshine Mountain, and she accepted readily, having found most of the runs on her initial visit much to her liking.

Mike accompanied them in Lance's rented car, but once there, took off on his own, leaving the two of them to share the rest of the day together. Haley was impressed with Lance's athletic prowess, and at times had trouble keeping up with his pace. By noon she was thoroughly spent, in need of a hearty lunch and something warm to thaw out the cold that had chilled her to the bone.

They ate in the summit restaurant, a noisy, crowded place that served a rather extensive menu, cafeteria-style. Haley found herself enjoying the ensuing conversation, listening with unsupressed interest as Lance recounted previous skiing adventures.

The remainder of the afternoon was spent back out on the slopes, and after catching up with Mike, the three of them set out for Banff once more, agreeing to get together that evening for a night on the town.

Haley was exhausted from the day's exploits, yet she hated to beg off for that night. After a deep, dreamless two-hour nap, she awoke refreshed, and ready once more to get going.

Mike suggested a particular nightclub he was fond of, and Haley and Lance agreed gamely. It was a rather loud discotheque, as Haley had suspected it would be, and although it was not her favorite type of place for entertainment, she found herself enjoying it immensely.

Several of Mike's friends joined their table during the course of the evening, and Haley was kept occupied the entire time—the object of much ego-nourishing male attention. She was on her feet almost constantly, her cheeks aching from the constant strain of laughing and smiling.

It was not until much later that evening that she glimpsed a puzzled expression on Lance's shadowed features. She had been laughing heartily at one of Bob Beasley's never-ending jokes, wiping tears of mirth from the corner of one eye as she happened to glance toward the end of the table. Lance was staring at her, a strange, thoughtful stare as he lifted his glass of gin and tonic and sipped it.

For some indiscernable reason Haley felt her skin growing warm as a deep flush spread its way along the base of her neck upward, her cheeks burning as if she were standing too near a blazing fire.

The music, being played now by the requisite disc jockey in a center-stage booth, from which two strobe lights emanated, had finally taken on a slower tempo, the bittersweet guitar strains of one of Haley's favorite songs, "Lyin' Eyes," now filling the dance floor with elbow-jostling couples. Rick, one of the guys in the group, stood up, moved toward Haley and, placing a hand on her forearm, mouthed an invitation for her to dance.

Haley managed to disengage her eyes from the heart-quickening stare that Lance was sending her way and she turned to indicate her acceptance of Rick's request. She stood up, but before she knew what was happening, her left hand was being encased in a larger, engulfing one, its firm grip demanding and possessive.

Haley looked up to see Lance standing next to her, sending a friendly but meaningful expression Rick's way.

The message was immediately understood by the young man as he swiftly withdrew and disappeared into the crowded room, no doubt in search of a more available partner.

Haley followed along behind Lance as he threaded a path through the crowded dance floor; he stopped as he found a small spot along the edge and pulled her toward him.. From the moment Haley felt her body being molded against the long length of his, her cheek turning to fit as snugly as hand in glove in the hollow beneath his collarbone, she was aware of her valiant resolution earlier in the week—carried out so far with such success—coming to naught.

Once again she found herself being swept away in a torrent of emotions as their bodies swayed to the slow beat and the tender soul-rending strains of the music; a melody that brought back all the heartbreak she had struggled so hard to put behind her. One of Lance's hands slipped beneath the cascade of auburn curls, wrapping itself around the base of Haley's neck. Instinctively her hand, which had been positioned on the outer corner of his shoulder, slid down and across the breadth of his back, relishing the granitelike hardness of the muscles beneath her gently kneading fingers.

The smell of the man was intoxicating; it dissolved any remaining reserves Haley might have had against letting herself fall into the trap of her physical desire for him.

As the song was replaced by yet another slow melody, Haley was besieged by an overwhelming fear that she had lost the only asset she had hoped to retain—her control over the sexual magnetism between herself and Lance. It was too strong, bigger than she, and much too tantalizing for her willpower to resist.

Lance had said not a word to her since leading her out onto the dance floor, but now he drew back the curtain of her hair, placing his mouth just beyond her cheek, his voice, when he spoke, sending currents of warm, moist air rushing along the inner recesses of her ear.

"How long did you think you could keep it up?" he asked, moving his lips a bit closer, his teeth closing gently over the soft flesh of her earlobe.

Haley drew her head back to answer him, but her "Keep what up?" was barely out before he firmly pressed her head once more against his chest.

"Teasing me all night with your flirting and sexy dancing with every man who asked you." His tone

118

was husky and accusing, yet with no overtones of discernible anger.

Nevertheless, the accusation set off a dangerous thrill in Haley, setting her nerve endings afire with a blaze of raw desire.

Considering his almost aloof attitude toward her this past week, Haley found it incredible that Lance was reacting to her this way tonight. The possibility that he had perhaps been holding it all in only served to make his sudden renewed interest all the more exciting and stimulating. Once more she tried to pull her head back, but it was useless to object, for Lance was playing the game his way. As they swayed together in rhythm with the music he held her smotheringly close; her breathing became increasingly labored. But Haley was oblivious to the discomfort, her heart tripping at an alarming rate as she hung on his every seductive word.

"Just keep quiet," he whispered in rasping tones. "The innocent act is over tonight."

Haley's breath caught as his hands spanned the narrow circumference of her waist, thumbs moving in sensuously stimulating circles, concentric waves of sheer desire rippling throughout the length and breadth of her body.

"I think we've put up with this charade long enough," he added, sounding suddenly impatient as he abruptly released her, keeping a firm hold on one of her hands as he led her back to their table.

Haley was grateful for the dimness of the discotheque, which mercifully hid the pinkish hue that now covered her face and neck. She waited behind Lance as he bent forward to speak to Mike for a moment, then nodded and turned back to her. Mike and the others at the table said good night to them both, and Haley returned the farewell just as Lance gave a hefty tug on her hand, leading her through the maze of tables, couches, and gyrating bodies.

Before stepping outside, Lance helped Haley into her jacket, then slid into his own. The clean night air and the relative quiet, after they emerged from the din and the smoke, was like jumping into a pool of ice water after a hot sauna. Both of them felt the refreshing sting of it, and their steps increased to an almost jaunty pace, Lance's arm glued possessively to Haley's coat-clad back.

"Where are we going?" Haley had to ask, knowing full well the answer.

Lance merely slanted a narrowed look down at her, his steps increasing almost twofold to hers.

They reached the car quickly, and after letting Haley in on the passenger side, Lance rounded the car and slid his long frame behind the wheel, pressing repeatedly with his boot against the accelerator, revving the cold engine before putting the car in reverse and heading it out toward the tiny parking lot exit.

Neither spoke during the ride back to the hotel, Haley fixing her gaze on the scenery flicking past her window, willing her nervous anticipation to a calmer state. It was a futile attempt, though, as her heartbeat quickened to an even faster rate when Lance reached for her hand, which, until now, had lain carefully folded into the other in her lap. He tugged on it gently until she slid across the seat closer to him. His eyes never leaving the road, he released her hand and placed his arm around her shoulders, his fingers kneading her upper arm through her jacket, sending shivers of expectation curling up and down her spine.

After parking the car in the hotel's covered parking area, the two of them made their way to the lobby, walking at a leisurely pace toward the elevators. Haley said nothing as she heard Lance ask the operator for his floor, not hers. Her nerves were tingling, though, as she strained against the full contemplation of what she was about to do.

Some vague voice within her made a halfhearted attempt at objecting, but it was silenced quickly as a much stronger, determined one made itself heard. Whatever pangs of conscience she might now be suffering were totally useless at this point, the voice asserted. Somewhere, deep inside, she had known that it would come to this eventually. Lance had always overruled even her most strident objections to this longing she was helpless to control.

Nothing had changed that undeniable fact.

CHAPTER EIGHT

As they walked down the hushed corridor toward his room, Lance glanced at his wristwatch.

"Hmmm," he muttered, "Just in time."

"What?" Haley glanced up at him curiously.

Stopping just outside his door, Lance withdrew his key from his jacket, saying, "There's something I think you'd enjoy seeing." He pushed open the door, and Haley walked into the room, wondering just what in the world he was referring to so mysteriously. Her bafflement was heightened when Lance failed to turn on any lights in the room, and, taking her by the hand, led her toward the window.

Haley's room was located on the opposite side of the enormous multileveled hotel, her window facing the rear grounds. As Lance drew back the curtains she looked out eagerly upon the magnificent view directly below. Easily visible was the crescent-curved drive on which she and the others had ridden that first night there. The view was as exhilarating as that one had been, though from a different perspective.

Gaslit lamps spread golden shadows across the snow-enshrouded landscape, the white-fringed blue-black forest beyond the circular drive completing the picture postcard setting to magical perfection.

"Isn't it wonderful?" Haley asked in an almost reverent tone.

Lance placed both hands just inside the lapels of

her jacket. "Why don't you take this off? I left the heat on, so the room should be comfortable."

"Of course," Haley answered, shrugging out of the coat and letting Lance dispose of it for the time being. She hugged both arms around her abdomen and turned to gaze back upon the lovely setting below.

Lance joined her once more, the solid length of each of his arms engulfing her, surrounding her with a warmth that seemed to permeate every fiber of her being.

"Ah, good," he muttered, his chin moving against the top of her head where it rested. "Here they come."

"Wha—" Haley began, then stopped, her mouth remaining parted with the half-formed word as she caught sight of what Lance was referring to. Just coming into view from the bend in the drive that entered the hotel proper from the forested grounds beyond, was a horse-drawn sleigh, the musical tinkling of its bells announcing its arrival. As it drew up to the front entrance door Haley watched in delight as the properly liveried driver alighted, helping the passengers—a man and woman—step down from their blanket-covered perch on the red leather seat. The two magnificent-looking white trotters stamped impatiently, their snorts sending streams of vapor into the frigid night air.

"Isn't it lovely?" Haley spoke in a hushed tone, lifting her head to glance up at Lance. "A horse-drawn sleigh. You know, I've never seen one other than in the movies or on television."

"How would you like to take a ride in one?" Lance asked.

"Is it possible?" Haley asked, feeling childlike in her excitement at the prospect.

"Anything is possible, if you set your mind to it," Lance said, meaningfully.

"Really?" Haley said, missing Lance's implication. "That would be great! A genuine horse-drawn sleigh."

"Then say no more," Lance said firmly, moving his hands to her shoulders and turning her toward him. He smiled down at her, and Haley's heart leaped at the sight of his moonlight-silhouetted features. He was so incredibly handsome, so virily masculine. He was all most women would ever require in a man, she mused, letting her hands wander upward, her fingers freely sliding through the wealth of gently curling locks. Slowly his lips descended toward her upturned face, her lips parting slightly as they felt the warm sweetness that had once known every part of her sensual being.

Her body swayed helplessly against the long length of his, feeling at once the primal need of him, the urgency that was beginning to rapidly consume her as well. Their kiss seemed never-ending: a devouring, insatiable prelude to what they both knew would finally satiate their long-ignored hunger for each other.

Haley was captive of her desire for Lance now, knowing very well what she had agreed to by coming here to his room tonight. She wanted him as much as he wanted her; that fact was uncontestable. Yet, as Lance's hands stroked the muscles of her upper arm, his fingers sliding along her shoulders to caress the smooth column of her throat, gingerly working their way down to rest above the gentle swell of her full breasts, that same inner voice made itself heard, desperately attempting one last protest.

Barely suppressing a groan that came from the depths of her being, she was able to pull away, her breathing coming in ragged spurts as she forced herself to give vent to nagging doubts and self-recriminations.

"Lance?" Her voice broke as she spoke his name.

"Hmmm?" He was nibbling now at the tender, sensitive skin below her ear, his hands having moved downward to cup the fullness of each breast.

Shuddering, she forced the question out. "I—I don't know—" She halted, unsure of how to put into words what was still plaguing her.

"What don't you know?" Lance answered, his tone husky with barely controlled desire. His fingers were methodically opening each of the buttons of her blouse, the material giving way as rapidly as her willpower was fading.

"I—I'm not sure what we're doing . . . is right," she finally managed.

"What's wrong with what we're doing?" he came back, slipping the bothersome blouse off her shoulders and down her arms, his hands returning to unhook the fastening of her bra.

She could have stopped then, stopped her protesting of what she wanted and needed with her entire soul. But still the voice within made its insistent demand, urging her to speak of her lingering doubts.

"It's not fair," she said weakly, her insides turning

to jelly as her bra was discarded, and his hands once more found the treasure of her swelling, achingly stimulated breasts. "What we're doing isn't fair," she repeated hoarsely.

"Fair to whom?" Lance questioned, raw desire playing havoc with the resonant timbre of his voice. "You don't seem to be objecting—at least physically. And I'm certainly not."

"I don't mean to us," she answered in an even shakier tone. "I mean . . . to Julia."

With that Lance's head snapped up, his hands, having now found their way to the waistband of her slacks, going rigid, as did his entire stance.

"Of all the—" he muttered exasperatedly. "Dammit, Haley. How can you even bring up that bitch's name at a time like this?"

Haley's response stuck in her throat, and she flinched at the harshness of his tone. The ensuing silence was broken as Lance spoke, his voice lower, calmer. "I thought you wanted to start over. I thought we weren't going to pick up where we left off. Isn't that what you said?"

Haley made no reply, swallowing deeply as she looked away.

"Well, isn't it?" Lance insisted softly.

"Yes," she answered finally. "That is what I said. . . . I just meant—"

"I don't think you do know what you meant."

"That's not true," Haley objected feebly.

"Isn't it? You've been covering up pretty well these past few days, but it's still there, isn't it? You can't lay it to rest. About Julia. The way she really is—the way she always was."

126

Haley squeezed her eyes shut tightly, a burning constriction at the back of her throat threatening ominously. He was right, of course. She hadn't laid it to rest at all. She'd been hurt—tremendously. Hurt by what Lance had revealed about her supposed best friend. Her brain was a jumble of mixed emotions over the whole situation; she simply wasn't prepared —or ready—to sort them out at this point.

As if reading her thoughts, Lance placed an arm around her, pulling her closer to him. With one hand he smoothly stroked the soft tumble of auburn tresses, pressing his mouth against the crown of her head.

"It's all right, babe. I understand. More than you'll ever know."

Haley began crying silently, her tears moistening the fuzzy wool of his sweater. Lance continued to stroke her hair, gently kissing the wispy tendrils around her forehead until her weeping abated.

"You know," he said in a lighter tone, "dreams really do die hard, don't they? But you'll get over it. One day you'll forget her completely."

Haley sniffed and licked one wet corner of her mouth. "Do you really believe that?"

"Yes, I do. We both made mistakes about Julia, Haley. And we can both be free of them someday. We *will*."

A dim light of hope grew within Haley at that moment; she could believe Lance, she really could. And someday she would forget her childish perception of a friendship that had existed really only in her mind, and she *would* recover from the hurt, the awkward embarrassment of a wounded ego.

Lifting her head, she smiled as Lance's fingers wiped away the last of her tears, then lowered his mouth to hers, softly, persuasively molding his lips against hers, plying them gently with the tip of his tongue until Haley opened them willingly, wantonly.

Haley found herself being returned rapidly into a vortex of mind-consuming physical response. Finally pulling away, and with inexorable patience on his part, Lance removed her clothing piece by piece until she stood naked before him. Lance stepped backward, and his breath caught audibly as his eyes roamed the length of her soft, supple curves, a visual lovemaking that sent a torrid fire snapping along every nerve in her body.

"Come here." He uttered the words on a groan, taking her by the hands and sitting on the side of the bed, pulling her alongside him as one hand clamped over his belt buckle, yanking back the leather strap. The sliding sound it made created a weak, quivering sensation in the center of her abdomen.

Haley lay back as Lance stood once more, watching the play of the moon's silvery light dancing across the rippling play of muscles that were exposed as he undressed. Her eyes were riveted on the hard, potent length of him, the exquisitely masculine body that she had never, in all the long, long months behind her, ever forgotten. He was every inch a male animal, just as she remembered him. As he came to her, lowering himself next to her on the narrow bed, she reached out for him, hungering for the feel of his flesh against her own. As his strong, tautly muscled arms pulled her next to him, she drank in the distinct smell of him, her mouth opening to gently bite the flesh of his shoulder, tasting the smooth, salty skin that mingled now with her own.

Lance's lips gently played along the soft hair of the crown of her head, moving slowly down the side of her neck, his tongue darting quickly, teasingly along the labyrinthine smoothness of her ear. A tiny groan escaped Haley's throat, and her fingers gripped instinctively into the sinewy muscles of his shoulders. Her mouth sought his, but he wasn't ready yet; he was enjoying far too much this rediscovery of the woman who had been there—in his dreams, his thoughts, his anguishing seizures of guilt ever since he had driven her from his life. The heat within him was almost too much to restrain, yet restraint was his as he slowly pleasured both himself and her with the warm, stirring caresses of his mouth and hands.

His lips were warm and moist now as they encountered the firm ridge of her jaw, tracing whisper-soft kisses over her cheeks, her nose, the tip of her chin, her closed eyelids. She shuddered beneath his touch, and when he placed the palm of his hand on one firm, ripe breast, its peak already hard and straining, the fire within him snapped dangerously, almost out of control.

Haley squirmed as his tongue flicked wetly across the rigid, burning nipple, and as her hands slipped down the length of his back, resting along either side of his flat waist, she found some measure of release in her own methodical, drugging massage.

Finally, with infinite tenderness and care, Lance moved above her, placing his lips against her ear as he whispered softly, "Do you want this, Haley? I want you to want this, too, you know."

How could he even ask it? she wondered wildly. She was crazy for him! Just as she had been all those months of trying to forget—ha! that was a laugh—all those months of struggling to begin her life anew.

She nodded, unaware she was doing so, and uttered a simple "Yes" as her hands slid carefully, longingly down his back, stopping to rest upon the swell of his hips, the firm, definitive pressure of her fingers against them answer enough.

His response was automatic, the fire leaping to its fullest, headiest flame now. Moving backward, he knelt for a moment above her, reaching down to caress her creamy, firm thighs, then gently, lovingly parting them. Placing his hands on the pillow on either side of her head, he lowered himself then, and when at last he moved to merge his body with hers, he heard her gasp as she thrust her hips upward to meet the pulsing rhythm that soon became her own.

It was a glorious, heady reunion of indestructable passion. Together, like this, they were whole, and Haley knew a joy she had thought belonged only to her past. Their lovemaking was sweet and pure, slow and rhythmically sensuous as they moved against and with and within one another: a magical symphony propelling them to dizzying heights of sheer ecstasy, its culmination so intense, it bespoke a power that went beyond what either could have possessed alone.

Haley shifted slightly, moving under the protective guard of Lance's arm to turn onto her side. She listened to his steady, even breathing, so dramatically different from the passionate cries of a while earlier. They had lain in one another's grasp for a while,

130

the heat of their passion slacking to a warm, tender glow that seemed to fuse them together. Neither would have even thought of leaving the bed in which they had loved one another so thoroughly, so lingeringly.

Filled with a peace that erased doubts and vague fears, Haley finally slept, too: a deep, bone-melting sleep that restored and replenished her body like no other she could recall. She awoke gradually, the sounds and smells reawakening her remembrance of the rapture of the night before. She snuggled closer within the cocoon of Lance's arms, smiling as his breath tickled the sensitive cord at the back of her neck. His mouth moved lower to nibble playfully along her shoulder, and Haley couldn't help but wriggle at the delightful sensations it was creating within.

"Aha," Lance muttered, his mouth pressed to the tangled locks of her auburn hair. "The sleeping princess awakens."

She rolled onto her side to face him, her own arms wrapping around his chest. "Mmm-mm," she answered, nuzzling her cheek against the rough night's growth of beard on his jaw and neck.

"Good," he said huskily, his hands beginning to stroke and caress her, igniting the spark of need within her to a leaping, crackling flame.

They rediscovered each other patiently this time, unlocking a wealth of sensations that promised even greater ones to be discovered. Haley delighted in the sight of Lance's hard, potent form, completely visible now in the pale morning light filtering through the window. As they became one, she knew only one

131

overwhelming conviction: whatever the consequences, however much she might live to regret her
actions, for now, without doubt, they seemed right
and just and completely fair to the only two people
in the world who would ever know about them.

As Haley was later to reflect, the reuniting of their
physical passion for each other was the launching of
a new relationship between them. For her part she
had never doubted her love for Lance, although she
had struggled against undefeatable odds to overcome
it. That same love for him had now been strengthened beyond her wildest imaginings, filling her with
an almost reverent joy, an emotion that colored her
every thought and deed.

For now her love alone was reason enough for
Haley to give credence to their renewed relationship.
It was more than obvious that Lance did care for her
in more than a purely physical sense; any declaration
of love on his part would merely be icing on the cake
of her rediscovered contentment with life.

From here on they shared every available moment
together, making the most of this magical, seemingly
endless fairy tale of reawakened passion. The beautiful, sparkling weather beckoned them outdoors, and
they spent all day Sunday skiing the slopes of Sunshine Mountain, Mount Norquay, and Lake Louise.
Lance was an expert skier, but Haley's own prowess
was not lacking; they kept up with each other handily.

On Sunday evening Lance made good his promise
to take Haley on the horse-drawn sleigh ride. She
had dressed warmly for the fifteen-minute drive

through the winding forest roads to the alpine-style restaurant, but the heavy plaid blanket Lance threw over them both was definitely helpful. Haley thought she could have withstood any degree of frigid weather, however; she was having an absolutely marvelous time.

She felt the pressure of Lance's fingertips through their gloves as he squeezed her hand, and she looked up at him, her amber eyes reflecting the clear moonlight as she said, "Thank you, Lance."

"For what?" His eyebrows raised slightly, and Haley's breath caught in her throat as the physical reality of his nearness shot through her. Automatically she snuggled closer to him beneath the blanket. Her gaze shifted forward to the driver seated high above them, the majestically formed Percherons, their bells tingling musically in the crisp night air.

"For thinking of this," she said, her breath lingering frostily upon her lips.

Lance lowered his head to kiss one cool, reddened cheek. "No thanks are needed." He paused, then said, "Tell me something. Are you happy?"

Haley looked at him in open surprise. "How can you even ask that? Of course, I'm happy."

Lance studied her thoughtfully, then pulled her even closer toward him. "Good. That's all I need to hear."

Haley rested her head against his shoulder, and she made no reply. How could she not be happy when she was with him like this? It was as though they were frozen into this space and time—a time that would exist, for her, forever.

Their lovemaking that night was tenderly patient,

an exercise in delicious restraint. Haley felt as though she had never been this alive, this aware of the sensations her body was capable of and which Lance summoned forth so expertly. He seemed to find unceasing delight in titillating her every nerve ending, every secret reservoir of passion, taking her over and over again—with his hands, his mouth, his own throbbing need—to the pinnacle of desire. Throughout the night theirs was a delicate kindling slowly building its licking, scorching flames into a rampaging fire of mutual desire and physical response, a response that could accept no substitute.

Haley slept peacefully beside Lance, secure in the magical timelessness of the moment, unafraid and heedless of the uncertain future that lay before them.

On Monday the first of the deliveries arrived, and she was consumed with the details of installing the artwork that began to add just the color and life she had been seeking.

With Lance's permission she had hired temporary help to assist her, yet, she still found herself embroiled in every minute detail of the project. By the week's end, her days occupied by work and her nights a continuation of the rapture she and Lance shared so wonderously, Haley was startled at the realization that Christmas Eve was upon them.

She and Lance decided to turn down Mike's invitation to a party, opting instead for a quiet celebration of the occasion in the very place that had brought them back together. The largest of the hotel's three dining rooms was hosting a special supper which, according to Lance, was an occasion in itself.

Indeed it was, Haley admitted as she and Lance dined on a meal such as she had never before experienced: succulent roast goose, chestnut dressing, and heavenly plum pudding mere highlights of the superbly prepared seven-course supper.

Adding to her delight, as much as to everyone else's in the capacity-filled dining room, was the surprising visit of a troup of kilt-clad bagpipe players, filling the air with their hauntingly beautiful melodies as they filed through the maze of candlelit tables. A resounding series of *Ho-ho-ho*'s followed in their wake as the most realistic-looking Santa Claus Haley had ever seen brought up the rear, his lumbering gate no doubt caused as much by the enormous white sack slung behind one shoulder as his girth.

Haley's spirits were soaring—as much from the heady, fun-filled atmosphere as the potent cognac that had followed the sumptuous meal. The two of them left the restaurant, Haley walking within the secure circle of Lance's arm wrapped around her, eager to discover where he was leading her so insistently. They moved down the wide corridor of the level on which the restaurant and two of the pubs were located, continuing across the connecting walkway to halt on a heretofore hidden balcony.

Haley gasped in delight at the scene that was unfolding. The cavernous stone-walled room below them—graced on three sides with twinkling, colorfully decorated Christmas trees—was bursting with joy and excitement exhibited by a youthful crowd waiting in unsuppressable anticipation.

"What is it? What's going on down there?" Haley asked, sounding as excited as the squirming, jumpy children below, all of whom were completely oblivious to their parents' admonitions to remain calm.

"You'll see," Lance answered, obviously enjoying the spectacle as much as she.

With his words the enchanting strains of the bagpipes sounded even closer. As both of them looked on, the brigade marched into the room, accompanied by squeals and shouts as Santa entered behind them, greeting them all with his booming, cheerful voice, his hand arcing in the air in a salute to them all.

As Santa covered the distance down the center aisle to the elevated stand at the front of the room, he heaved his enormous bag up and around his shoulder, dropping it onto the floor. He took his seat in an enormous throne made especially for him, calling out a jolly "Merry Christmas" to each member of his expectant audience. Following a prearranged program, yet instilling it with the proper amount of authenticity, Santa began opening his sack, and with as much pomp as the circumstance deserved, began withdrawing an assortment of presents, calling out the names of the intended, handing them out individually as the children ran forward to receive them.

"What a wonderful idea!" Haley whispered enthusiastically. "Can you imagine what must be running through those little ones' heads?"

Lance chuckled. "Not a thing that isn't going through yours."

Haley smiled even as she frowned. "You don't have to make fun of me," she scolded lightly. "Is that why you brought me up here?"

"Of course not," Lance answered, pulling her closer and turning her toward him, surprising her by planting a resounding smack on her lips.

"What was that for?" Haley laughed, her amber eyes glowing brightly as she gazed up at him.

Lance gave an upward nod of his head. "Look above you."

Instantly, Haley lifted her eyes to observe a sprig of mistletoe dangling a few feet above them.

"That's why I brought you up here," he said, smiling wickedly.

"I see," Haley commented dryly. "So you've been scouting around, finding all the mistletoe. How clever."

He laughed and hugged her close. "*I* thought so. And there's plenty more to make use of. Follow me, young lady."

With a giggle Haley allowed herself to be pulled along, every bit as excited at each stop beneath the abundant mistletoe as the first.

Reflecting upon the event the next morning, Haley thought she couldn't have invented a more romantic Christmas setting, thinking that someday—when she had children of her own—she would love to bring them here. She could easily picture the sort of father Lance would make: patient, caring, attentive—a man with all the desirable characteristics of a loving parent.

At once Haley was taken aback at her own presumptuousness. Who was she to assume, or even imagine, that Lance would someday be a father? And Lord help her if she connected the possibility of that occasion to herself. No, such fantasizing would serve

137

no purpose except to remind her of a situation that was nothing more than an impossible dreamworld.

Christmas Day had been a lazy one, neither Haley nor Lance having the slightest urge to expend even an ounce of energy on any activity other than sharing each other's company.

Lance surprised Haley with a Christmas present: a maple leaf pendant bearing a single diamond in its center, held on a slender eighteen-karat gold chain. There was no doubt that she would cherish the gift for the rest of her life, no matter what the future held.

She had thought to purchase a gift for Lance, too, and he was pleased with the down-lined leather gloves, promising to wear them on their next ski excursion.

As the holidays wore on, she had to remind herself repeatedly of the fact that there was no guarantee that what she and Lance were sharing now could be continued upon their return home. It was a painful reminder: that this was merely a temporary situation, one made possible and fostered by the circumstances of the setting. She would be wise to heed the fact now, lest the truth hit her even harder later.

Yet, it was a difficult task she set herself; each moment they were together found her falling deeper and deeper in love with Lance. Why, oh why, she cursed the Fates, couldn't they have met earlier—before his involvment with Julia? What a difference it would have made in their lives—in all of their lives! In spite of the fact that they had agreed to begin their relationship anew, the past was still very much a part of the present. One thought of how Julia would react if she knew what was going on between her and

138

Lance confirmed that undeniable and unalterable fact. Lance might not see it that way, but then he didn't see his relationship with Haley the way she did either. Naturally he would shrug aside the influence his former relationship with Julia had on his new one with Haley. He had nothing to lose at this point, having already rid himself of an unhappy marriage to a woman who had merely been a burden to him these last couple of years.

And then there would always be that niggling doubt that Lance's work—his life—would come between them just as it had between him and Julia. He *was* a very ambitious man; Julia had been absolutely correct about that one facet of Lance's personality. Haley had no assurance whatsoever it would not stand in the way of a relationship with her.

It was all too possible Lance would not place that much at stake concerning their future relationship. But it was not the same for her, and it never would be. She was more in love with him than she could have ever imagined, the physical side of their relationship a mere extension of that love, and not, as it was to Lance, the primary consideration.

No, she must be very, very careful, she instructed herself repeatedly, forcing herself to remember each time her mind began its wanderings, that what she and Lance shared was only for now. She would be a reckless fool to bank on anything else.

Nevertheless, the remaining time before the New Year's Eve opening of the restaurant sneaked past them rapidly and brought them closer and closer. They revealed more and more of themselves to each other, sharing aspects of their personal selves that would have seemed impossible before.

Haley's shipment of the statuary piece from San Francisco finally arrived, and she was kept busy with its installation as well as taking care of the paperwork that seemed never-ending.

Every day now the restaurant was filled with employees receiving instructions from Mike as to their job requirements. Anticipation permeated the atmosphere, and Haley shared it, feeling as much a part of it as the rest of them.

The opening on New Year's Eve proved to be more than a satisfactory culmination of work well done. Lance was the epitome of romantic fulfillment to Haley that night—breathtakingly handsome in a well-fitted dark gray tweed suit. He never forgot her presence, though he tried to be everywhere at once, making certain that his pet enterprise was off to a fitting start.

Some of the guests present for the auspicious occasion knew Lance on a first-name basis, having dealt with him in the formative stages of the restaurant. He would introduce Haley in a most adoring manner, as if she were a prize he was proudly showing off.

And indeed, he had every right to do just that. Haley had taken pains to present an appropriately becoming appearance for the evening, and she was not at all displeased with the results of her efforts. Her lapis-colored V-neck gown swathed her snugly, revealing a curvaceous, slender figure her usual bulky winter wear hid far too well. Yet, she remained unaware of the absolutely stunning picture she made, oblivious to the stares she drew from men and women alike, her attention focused on the object of her own affections: Lance.

Occasionally, however, her mind did wander to another, rather disruptive thought—that she would be leaving on Sunday, returning to Denver. She had hoped that she and Lance would be flying back together, but their reservations had been made separately, and her flight was completely booked by now. Their parting somehow filled her with a strange, almost silly sense of foreboding.

Determinedly she shrugged it aside, concentrating her energies on enjoying their remaining time together.

CHAPTER NINE

Her energies had been well spent, Haley reflected somberly, observing the billowing cumulous clouds through her window as the airplane made its ascent into the Canadian sky, heading southward toward Denver.

Reflecting back on it, her relationship with Lance had moved toward some higher level, drawing them closer, in as much a mental sense as a physical one. God, how she wanted to believe that. To her, at least, it was true—she couldn't have loved him any more. Yet, there were still lingering doubts about the prudence of letting herself hope for too much. Lance had never given any indication that there was any emotion deeper than an affection on his part.

He had promised to call as soon as he returned on Wednesday, and she hung on to that prospect tenaciously. It was all she had to fill the void his absence now created—a void deeper even than the long two and a half years apart from him.

Her thoughts chased round and round in a similar vein until she could not bear them a moment longer. Time seemed to drag as the airplane winged its long journey home, and she was hard put to keep herself sufficiently occupied. Even the movie—a love story —was reminiscent of her own unhappy state of affairs.

As the final leg of the flight was imminent, however, Haley did discover her thoughts taking a different course, a not unpleasant anticipation of her arrival. She was eager to see her family, hoping that her sister had stayed on a few days longer for the holidays. Then, too, she was eager to tackle her work, her first experience tucked securely under her belt this time, adding a wealth of credibility that would surely enhance her future prospects. The uncertainty of what was going to occur between her and Lance upon his return still nipped at the edge of her consciousness, but she was more willing and able now to let it ride. There was nothing she could do about it in the meantime, and she philosophized that unsolved problems sometimes had a way of working themselves out.

She could not have known, at that point, how accurate her philosophy would turn out to be. Her arrival back in Littleton was much more satisfying than she had anticipated. She hadn't realized how much she was ready to be back home. The sojourn in Banff had been the perfect length of time, although, she admitted, it would have been far too long a stay had she not been able to share the time with Lance.

At any rate she was thankful she'd had the foresight to install an answering device on her telephone. Her wearisome treks around the Denver metropolis had apparently come to some avail. She was pleasantly surprised at the number of messages requesting her return call. She would have loved to sit down then and there and begin working, but she would, of course, have to wait until the next day. Sunday was not exactly a day to make business calls, and besides, she planned on spending the remainder of it with her parents at their home.

As soon as she had unpacked the most necessary items, Haley showered and dressed and left the town house for the short drive to her parents'. Happy as she was to be with them, she couldn't help feeling a bit of disappointment that her sister had left the previous day.

"Honey, she really wanted to see you," Mrs. Jordenson explained, serving coffee in the den after supper. Mr. Jordenson's eyes at the moment were glued to the television set, totally absorbed by the sights and sounds of his favorite football game.

"But the girls will be starting back to school tomorrow, and she had too many things to do to get them ready."

"I understand," Haley said, sipping her cup of steaming coffee. "I just missed seeing everyone for Christmas—especially the girls. Every time I see them, they've grown another foot."

Mrs. Jordenson affirmed that with a chuckle and a nod. "You couldn't be more right about that. But," she said firmly, placing her cup on its saucer on the coffee table, "you promised to tell me all about Banff. I want to know everything—so how was it?"

Haley smiled at her mother's enthusiasm and began relating facts and incidents more pertinent to the business side of the trip, carefully leaving out any mention of the amount of time spent in Lance's company.

"Well, it certainly sounds as though you were kept busy. How did you like working for Lance, honey? Really?"

Cautiously masking any telltale signs of emotion, Haley answered as lightly as possible. "He's very easy to work with, actually. As a matter of fact, he gave me full rein, even as to the more dramatic, important pieces. I suppose he trusted my instincts more than his own."

"Hmmm," her mother muttered thoughtfully. She made a small clicking sound with her tongue as she pushed her glasses farther up the bridge of her nose. "By the way, I spoke to Mrs. Morris the other day. We ran into each other in a dress shop. I asked about Julia, and she said she had been released from the hospital last Monday."

Something sharp and stinging knifed through Haley's insides at the information her mother imparted so casually. Since Haley's return she hadn't given Julia a thought, a surprising fact, inasmuch as she had never been able to put her completely out of her thoughts the entire time she was in Banff. Her mother's mention of Lance's ex-wife now brought home with full force the real reason behind her insecurity as far as her own and Lance's future was concerned.

"How is she?" Haley asked, bringing her cup to her lips and aiming for a casual tone.

"Well, Mrs. Morris said she seems to have recovered completely. She is living with them, you know, and I think they've been trying to convince her to look into getting a job—something to keep her occupied and help her meet other people."

Haley gave a barely perceptible nod. "That sounds like a good idea. She needs to get involved with something other than her own problems."

"I agree," Rita Jordenson stated firmly. "I'm sure

145

she also could use a few friends to help her over this lonely period in her life." She cast her daughter a meaningful glance.

"Perhaps you should call her, Haley," she said. "In fact," she added somewhat sheepishly, "I took the liberty of telling Mrs. Morris that you would when you got back."

With utmost difficulty Haley hid the amazement she felt at her mother's words, but she was hard put to prevent the irritation she felt from seeping into her reply.

She gave a brief sigh. "Mother, I wish you wouldn't have," she said tightly.

Mrs. Jordenson seemed taken aback at her daughter's reaction. "Honey, I didn't think I was interfering in your life by doing so," she said apologetically. "I just know how worried Mrs. Morris must be— although she hides her feelings fairly well. I was just trying to comfort her by suggesting that you could possibly offer support for Julia."

Haley said nothing, focusing her amber gaze on the rim of her cup, which she now held in both hands. She mulled over her mother's words, not at all sure how to explain her reticence about carrying out her mother's well-meaning offer. She couldn't begin to tell her the truth. Her mother's reaction to the entire story behind Julia's marriage to Lance would be too much to handle; she hadn't as yet learned to cope with her own lingering trauma.

"I understand," she said finally. "It's just that— well, Julia and I aren't exactly friends like we used to be. We didn't see each other for over two years, you know."

"Of course, dear, but you were so close—best friends for all those years you were growing up. You both just need to get reacquainted." Mrs. Jordenson's voice dropped to a softer, maternal tone. "I'm sure you could do her a world of good, Haley."

Once again Haley was forced to hide her irritation, her mother's demanding tone setting her on edge. She was being forced into a corner, a tactic her mother didn't often try with her. Why, of all things, did she have to choose this painful subject to pursue?

"All right," Haley said, forcing an agreeable tone into her voice. She shrugged one shoulder. "I'll give her a call, but I really don't think it will impress her. Not after the way she acted in the hospital. She couldn't have cared less if I was there or not."

If that were only true, Haley mourned silently. But indeed, the case was just the opposite. It had all been a carefully executed charade designed to lead Haley astray, to make her believe—even now—that Julia had known nothing about her affair with Lance. But why? The agonizing question begged to be answered.

Inwardly Haley felt a reverberation of some vague fear. She had no answer to the question, and truthfully she had no desire for one.

"I'm certain that was because she was so ill, dear," her mother insisted. "She was heavily sedated, her mother told me, and surely that, too, would have affected her behavior toward you."

"Maybe so," Haley conceded verbally, knowing too well that even drugs would not have had that much effect on Julia's extraordinary performance that day. Not considering the sort of scenes she had been capable of before.

147

Ignoring her mother's desire to continue the conversation, Haley stood up, moving toward her father's chair and placing one hand on the back of it.

"What's the score now, Dad?" she asked pointedly, realizing she might be offending her mother, but eager to switch the subject anyway.

Taking a chair next to her father's, she sat through the rest of the game with him; Mr. Jordenson was pleased to have someone with whom to share his own armchair football strategies. Rita Jordenson apparently took no offense at her daughter's unwillingness to continue a discussion she thought interesting enough. She was satisfied that Haley had agreed to contact her old friend. Things could take care of themselves from that point on.

By the time Haley took her leave that night, the disturbing conversation about Julia was pushed conveniently to the back of her mind. As long as her mother believed that she would call her old friend, she was safe. She hoped the subject would be dropped, but even if it wasn't, she could always think of a little white lie to cover up the fact that she had no intention whatsoever of carrying out Mrs. Jordenson's promise to Julia's mother.

As it turned out, Mrs. Jordenson's well-meaning suggestion that Haley contact Julia was unnecessary. Julia herself took the initiative—arriving on Haley's doorstep only minutes after Haley's return home on Monday evening.

The day had been long and tiring, albeit a most rewarding one. Haley had made her calls that morning, managing to arrange for two interviews that afternoon. One had turned out to be a fairly lucrative offer, and she had accepted on the spot. She had agreed to draw up a proposal for an art program that would upgrade and update the existing design of several floors of a well-known public relations business, located in a downtown Denver office complex.

Haley's head was spinning with ideas, and the only other thought that surpassed her preoccupation with this new, highly interesting prospect was that Lance would be arriving back in Littleton in two days. The thought of it filled her with a strange mixture of emotions: happiness, excitement, and more than a small amount of dread. She longed to see him with her entire being, she couldn't deny it. But she was stricken with a feeling akin to panic that something would happen to prevent a continuation of their seeing each other.

She couldn't help but imagine the worst possibility: perhaps it was not meant to be that the affair they had resumed within the privacy and solitude of Banff should continue here. Would "tempting the Fates" be too strong a term to apply to the situation? Haley wondered. Her love for Lance had come to naught here in Littleton two and a half years ago. Why should it have more of a possibility of surviving now?

Her mind torn between the conflicting thoughts about her job and Lance's pending arrival, Haley hung her heavy overcoat in the downstairs closet. She wondered who would be ringing at her door at this time of day. Probably her mother, she reasoned.

"Just a minute," she called out, running her fingers along her nape, freeing the auburn tresses that had been flattened from the wool hat and scarf binding them close to her head.

Reaching the front door, she unlocked the bolt, opened it slightly, and peered round to see who was there. The figure standing outside was turned away from her, so completely bundled up that Haley still had no idea who her visitor was.

"Yes?" she questioned, keeping her hand on the chain latch before completely opening the door.

Unconsciously her mouth parted slightly as the figure turned, revealing all too clearly her astonishment at Julia's presence on her doorstep. Julia, however, seemed quite at ease, her blue-green eyes glinting bemusedly at Haley's reaction.

"Hello," Julia said, smiling cheerfully. "I was hoping you'd be home."

Haley gulped, reluctantly sliding open the chain lock and pulling back the door. "Hello, Julia," she said quietly, mentally assessing what this surprise visit was all about. Instantly on guard, she was unsure how to handle the situation. Despite the forebodings she'd experienced since being home, though, she had not once considered the possibility of this.

"Aren't you going to ask me in?" Julia asked coyly, her eyes sparkling with false vivacity.

There was nothing else to do but just that, Haley realized. She was stuck; perhaps, she mused, it was for the best. If she and Julia were going to have things out, it would be just as well to get it over with now. Mustering every last vestige of courage, Haley managed a weak smile, stepping back to make room for Julia's entrance.

"Of course," she said evenly. "Come in."

"Brrr!" Julia exclaimed, sashaying past Haley, quite the picture of health. She was not at all the pitiable creature she'd presented only a few weeks ago in the hospital. "It's ridiculously cold today. Winter's only half over, and I'm already wishing for spring."

"May I take your coat?" Haley asked, covering her impatience with Julia's apparent desire for a requisite amount of small talk before she got down to what was really on her mind.

"Yes, please," Julia replied sweetly, shrugging out of her sporty, white fur jacket and handing it to Haley.

"Lovely jacket," Haley commented, walking toward the small entrance closet to hang it up. She might as well do her part in this little charade, she thought dryly.

"Thank you. I really love it." Julia fluffed out her shoulder-length blond locks and plopped down in a wingback chair, as casually as if she visited every day. "Actually it was a present from Lance," she added. "For my birthday, the first year we were married."

Haley maintained a polite expression as she walked toward the kitchen. She'd arrived home ravenously hungry after the long day, but at the present she could stomach only something warm to drink.

"Would you like a cup of coffee? Or tea, perhaps?"

"Oh, no, thanks," Julia answered, picking up a magazine from the coffee table and starting to leaf through it. "Go ahead if you want some. Don't mind me."

As if that were possible, Haley retorted silently.

151

"So, what brings you to this part of Littleton?" she asked in her most laconic tone, a feat not so easily accomplished. She was becoming increasingly uncomfortable with Julia's presence here. No—increasingly *nervous* would be a more accurate description.

"Some shopping," Julia answered lightly, lingering over fashion pages that caught her eye as she continued her perusal of the magazine. "And you, of course."

Haley's head snapped up at that last remark, grateful that her back was turned as she placed the kettle of water on the range burner.

"I've been wanting to see your place since you came back, and I thought today would be a nice day to drop in and have a little visit." Haley turned to see Julia look up. "Like old times, you know?"

What a ridiculous game, Haley thought, her hackles rising as she felt herself becoming almost defensive. She didn't want this woman in her house. Why didn't she simply throw her out? Something told her that that would more than likely prove an impossible feat.

"No. I *don't* know," Haley said, hearing herself sounding every bit as catty as Julia.

Julia pouted, her prettily painted mouth twisting cutely as she wrinkled up her nose. "Haley, you know how we used to be able to talk about *everything.*" The emphasis on the last word grated on Haley, and she clamped her teeth tightly as she leaned against the frame of the kitchen door, her arms crossed over her chest.

Nodding slightly, Haley raised a questioning eyebrow, hoping her stance was sufficient to indicate her lack of cooperation in the tack Julia was pursuing.

"So . . ." Julia began, smiling with feigned intrigue. "Tell me all about your new career."

"What do you want to know?" Haley asked, her icy tone belying an affable expression.

"Oh, everything," Julia gushed. "I don't really remember what we talked about in the hospital when you came to visit," she said apologetically. "So if you told me about it then, I don't have any recollection of it. However, Mom told me she spoke to your mother, and she said you were quite excited about it."

If Julia was in no hurry to get to the point, Haley thought, then she wasn't going to help her get there.

"Yes, I am," Haley said. "Today, in fact, was a very promising day for me. I received two interested offers, and I'm fairly certain I'll receive a contract on one."

"How *nice*," Julia exaggerated.

Haley wondered how in the world the friendship between the two of them had ever lasted as long as it had. Had she changed that much, that she only now saw those qualities in Julia that were positively distasteful? Or was it Julia who had changed, her naturally flighty personality hardening into one of bitter cynicism that bore no resemblance to her former self?

"But I was referring to your job in Banff," Julia went on smoothly. "How did it go?"

"Very well," Haley answered, playing right along. "I must say it provided a feather in my cap."

"And how did you enjoy working for Lance?"

Julia asked. Even from her position several feet away, Haley was sure she detected a muscle twitching in Julia's jaw.

"It went very well, as a matter of fact," Haley replied. "How did you know about it?"

Julia produced a plastic smile. "My dear mother, as I'm sure you remember, never misses a thing that goes on in this community. Your mother told her about it, and naturally she told me."

"I see."

"You were there for quite a while," Julia commented. "Do you expect all your jobs to take that long? I mean, is that the standard for what you'll be doing?"

Her roundabout questioning did not hide the issue at stake, but Haley decided she could be just as vague as Julia.

"No, as a matter of fact, it's not," she answered. "Most jobs I'll be handling—or those I hope to be handling—won't require near as much time. This one did, though, because of an important piece of artwork that was back-ordered. I wanted to be there to see to its proper installation."

"Oh, I don't blame you," Julia said. "I suppose you got in some skiing while you were there too."

"Yes. It was very nice."

Haley could feel the tension between the two of them hanging in the air like a humid, oppressive front preceding a pending storm. She felt smothered by it, her pulse quickening as the expression in her amber eyes hardened them into two dark topaz stones.

"And how about Lance?" Julia asked, not bothering now to feign an innocent tone. "Did he enjoy himself?"

"I imagine so," Haley answered noncomittally.

"I hope he didn't work himself too hard," Julia commented. "He's fanatical about his restaurant business, you know." She was glaring now, and Haley was truly shaken by the strange, undefinable glint in her blue-green eyes.

"He fits the definition of a workaholic to a T." Abruptly she heaved a sigh of exasperation. "I swear, it would take something earthshaking to get that man's mind on something else, you know? And I'd love to be the one to make it happen," she said in low, menacing tone.

Haley offered no comment, merely widening her eyes as if to say she had no idea about the subject. The woman obviously cherished a fantasy of revenge. Haley certainly had no wish to hear any more. She was itching for Julia to leave now, hoping the telephone would ring so she would have an excuse to cut short this ludicrous visit. Evidently Julia was not going to bring up the issue of Haley and Lance's affair. Did she still think that Haley didn't know of her knowledge of it? Was she still merely trying to make Haley as uncomfortable as possible by keeping her on the edge of her seat?

At this point Haley was past caring about Julia's motives. All she could think of was how in the world to get rid of her. Lacking a clever device, she would have to resort to bluntness.

Pointedly she walked into the living room and glanced at the wall clock.

"Good Lord, it's almost seven o'clock," Haley

said, returning to the kitchen and opening the refrigerator, pulling out lettuce and other makings of the salad that was to be her supper. She doubted, however, that she'd have the appetite to down it after this episode.

"I really hate to sound rude, Julia," she said, mustering an apologetic tone, "but I've got a load of things to take care of before the night is over, and tomorrow is going to be just like today—long and strenuous."

Taking the hint with mock graciousness, Julia stood up. "Oh, I'm sorry I've been keeping you. However, I'm glad I dropped by." She gave a brief sweep of the room with her eyes. "You really do have a lovely place."

"Thank you," Haley replied, walking back toward the closet and retrieving Julia's coat. "I'm very happy with it."

Julia accepted the coat, and pushed her arms through, bending over to pick up her purse, which she had placed on the butler's table when she came in.

Haley was at the door, hand on the knob, ready to open it. As Julia walked toward it she hesitated, inclining her head to one side, the frozen expression on her face indicating the game was now over. "It won't work, you know. You'll be making a serious mistake if you think it will. Take it from someone who's been there."

Haley's stomach flipped at the tone in Julia's voice, but she held on to her fragile control over the anger about to explode momentarily.

"Excuse me, but I have no idea what you're talking about," she said, barely suppressing the quivering that was rapidly spreading from her voice to the rest of her body.

"I think you do," Julia countered, walking past Haley and out onto the doorstep. Haley wondered later why she hadn't slammed the door that very instant.

"I'm only telling you this for your own good," Julia said sympathetically. "I don't think you're the type that could handle a man"—her voice dropped as she added—"like Lance, that is. His work is everything to him. It always has been and it always will be. Believe me, I know more about that man than you'll ever hope to." She smiled condescendingly. "And I do hope for your sake, Haley, that you'll think seriously about it. I'd hate to see you get hurt the way I was."

She pulled one hand from the furry pocket of her jacket and raised it, smiling falsely as she made a tiny waving gesture. "Call me soon, okay? Bye now," she called out over her shoulder as she opened the wooden patio door and disappeared around it.

Haley gave the door a hefty shove at that point, the sound reverberating throughout the town house, causing one small painting hung in the entry hall to jump on its hook.

Raging inwardly, Haley slumped her back against the door, alarmed at the racing of her heart.

She couldn't recall ever having experienced such fury, such soul-burning resentment toward one person. It seemed incredible, but she could almost believe that she actually hated the woman, an emotion she thought would never enter the realm of her life.

Why couldn't Julia have just come right out and laid her cards on the table? Why couldn't she admit that she had always known about Lance's affair with her? Why couldn't the two of them have discussed the whole sorry matter like two rational adults? No, it had to be some game, some ridiculously silly game that ended with Julia's veiling her own hatred for Haley with bitter innuendos.

Haley brought a hand up to her brow, spreading her fingers and rubbing them in slow circles against her temples, in which by now a dull throbbing had begun. She drew in a deep breath and let it out slowly. Whom was she trying to fool? she questioned herself silently. Certainly not herself. She could have forced Julia into an open no-holds-barred discussion as to what was really on both their minds. Why hadn't she?

Because she was afraid, that was why. Afraid of admitting to Julia her own love for Lance. Afraid of what Julia might say in that regard. But that wasn't reason enough, was it? Wasn't she simply reluctant to make a stand about her and Lance's relationship for fear it would make her appear foolish? Foolish because she would be basing everything on her own feelings? Wasn't the real issue here the fact that she couldn't stand up to Julia because she hadn't a thing to support her?

Trudging slowly toward the living room, she slumped down on the couch, propping her elbow on the end and cupping her chin within her palm. Dry-eyed, she stared out the bay window, her gaze fixed at some distant point beyond the wooden fence surrounding the private patio. She felt an overwhelming emptiness in the pit of her stomach, an emptiness that had now replaced the hunger pains.

It was true, she realized with a sickening impact. All she had was her love for Lance. He had never said he loved her, never told her that she was the most important part of his life and that he wanted to share that life with her as his wife. With a cold certainty she knew that his work was his real love, that it would always come first, just as it had when he was married to Julia. And maybe now that was all he really wanted, really needed.

That was precisely where Julia might have been right, Haley mused, her heart sinking at the prospect. She, regardless of her own undeniable physical desires, would never be able to handle having Lance on merely the terms that implied. She had no desire to take second place in his life—none whatsoever. And being his mistress was out of the question. Physical satisfaction could be found anywhere and anytime, and she had no doubt Lance would ever lack willing companionship in that department.

For herself, however, it would not—it could not— ever be enough. She loved the man, loved him too much always to remain on the outside of his life looking in. She needed to be a part of his life, a vital factor in it, as he was in hers. This was certainly not an original discovery, Haley realized. She had left him in the first place for that very reason. What had happened in Banff had been a brief remission, something she would never forget—indeed it would live with her forever. But it was a magical once-in-a-lifetime experience, and that was all.

How long she remained on the couch in the very

same position, Haley had no idea, but when she finally roused herself, she was stiff and overwhelmingly tired, feeling years older. So much to be taken care of tonight, she remembered vaguely, trudging slowly up the stairs, completely forgetting about the salad she had intended to eat.

The last thing she cared for at the moment was food. Her appetite had been destroyed when Julia had first arrived, her mere presence enough to eradicate any amount of hunger. But it was more than Julia's visit that had wreaked havoc on her digestive system, Haley admitted, swallowing back the lump forming in the back of her throat. It was the fact that, for the first time, she was really facing the way things had to be from now on. Her life—as much as she had hoped and prayed otherwise—would simply have to go on as before: alone, without Lance.

160

CHAPTER TEN

It was a harsh, cruel realization, but one about which Haley no longer harbored any further doubts. She and Lance were not meant to be together; the matter was as simple as that. He, of course, might object to her decision not to see him anymore, but that was the way things had to be from now on—if not for his sake, then for the sake of her own sanity.

Miraculously Haley managed to pull herself together, setting herself to the task of working up a proposal to be presented to the public-relations firm on Tuesday afternoon. Securing this particular project would enable her to consider her career well launched. Work was exactly what she would need from this point on. The more of it, the better.

Her proposal stood on its own merits, and Haley was pleased that she did indeed obtain a contract for her efforts. She was to start on the project as soon as possible, and with that thought in mind she made it through the night, shoving Lance's return home the next day as far back in her mind as was reasonably possible.

Sleep, however, did not come easily, and it was a fatigued-lined face that greeted her in the mirror the next morning. Lance was foremost in her mind despite the heavily scheduled day awaiting her, but there was little she could do about it until he called.

Haley had arrived home that evening later than

she'd planned, and for a rare few minutes, as she set about slapping together a sandwich to assuage the ravenous hunger she'd ignored most of the day, thoughts of Lance were completely absent. Thus, the ring of the telephone as she finished the first bite of her sandwich was a jolting sound, snapping her back to harsh reality.

She thought for a moment about ignoring the call, but, deciding that would be a coward's way out, she placed the barely eaten sandwich on her plate and stood, moving with visible trepidation to the telephone on the bar.

"Hello?" She gulped the greeting.

Lance's voice was smooth and sensual, the sound of it setting her veins aflame with a fire so potent, it fairly singed her entire system with the heat of it.

"Haley?" Lance sounded unsure, as if thinking perhaps he had dialed the wrong number.

"Yes. It's me," Haley answered, managing a more even tone.

"Is something the matter?" He sounded truly concerned.

"No," Haley answered. "I was starting to eat a sandwich. I suppose I didn't sound like myself."

Lance chuckled, the sound filling Haley with its warm low timbre. "You sure didn't! A sandwich," he added derisively. "I can take you out for something more subtantial than that."

"No, that's okay." The words rushed out, and Haley made a conscious effort to check her further reply. "Thank you, really, Lance. But I've had one heck of a day, and I don't think I could stand having to get all bundled up all over again."

"No problem. I'll bring something over. Be there, oh, say, half an hour."

Haley opened her mouth, the objection she was about to utter freezing on her tongue.

"Haley?"

"Yes?"

"Is something wrong? Are you sure you're all right?"

"N-no, I'm fine," she answered vaguely.

"Okay, then, see you in a little while."

Haley replaced the receiver in its cradle, staring at it for a long anxious moment. He was coming over! Reaching up, she wiped away a film of moisture above her upper lip. Then, standing straighter, she took a few steps, raising her head determinedly. Perhaps it would be better this way: get it over and done with and go on with her life. With a sinking sensation in the pit of her stomach she realized how dreadful even a contemplation of that life would be.

Lance walked through her front door with an air of familiarity that Haley found distinctly painful. His commanding presence, the overwhelming masculine aura he projected, so completely filled her cozy, singular abode with his presence that she was almost frightened by it. Setting down the bags containing cartons of Chinese food, he shucked out of his sheepskin jacket and let his gaze roam about the cleverly decorated downstairs.

"Nice," he commented. "Very nice." He cocked an eyebrow and smiled winningly at her. "But then, what else could one expect from a bona fide art consultant?"

Haley's silence caught his attention and he turned to face her. "Haley?" He spoke her name quizzically, frowning slightly as he saw that she had moved to the end of the bar and was staring blankly at the floor.

Lance moved toward her and placed his hands on her shoulders. Still, she refused to look at him, and he shook her slightly.

"Haley, look at me."

She did so finally, and he did not miss the telltale shininess of those golden irises, nor the ripple of flesh against her throat as she swallowed spasmodically.

"What is it, Haley? What's wrong?" His tone was uncompromising, and Haley knew she had to break physical contact to do what she must. Lifting her hands, she removed his own from her shoulders and walked past him into the living room. She crossed her arms over her chest and drew in a slow, shuddering breath. Lance's frown deepened to a scowl as he watched her, his impatience obvious in his stance.

"Answer me, Haley," he commanded. "I don't have time for whatever game it is you're up to."

"I—I just—" Her voice was weak, strangled. God, this was unbelievably difficult! Why did things have to be this way? Haley anguished, wishing for all the world that she didn't have to say it. But she had to. As painful as it was, it was the only thing to do.

"Lance, I don't think we should continue seeing each other. It won't work. . . . It—it can't. Not the way it worked in Banff. I think we'd be better off not to even start anything here."

"Oh?" His tone was dry, coldly cynical; she could picture the coolness in that gray-green gaze. Did he even give a damn? Haley wondered, angry that she should be experiencing such pain over the matter while he was simply taking it in stride. But it was a poor assessment of his reaction, she discovered quickly.

"It's as simple as that, is it? You simply presume to make that decision for both of us?"

"That's not what I'm doing," Haley objected, turning back abruptly to face him.

"Oh, really? Then what do you call it?" Lance's tone dripped sarcasm, and Haley cringed at the sound of it.

"Lance, you don't understand—"

"No, I don't think I do," he interrupted harshly, bitterness edging his voice now. "But, please . . . do continue." He still stood near the bar; yet, again Haley had the sensation that the entire room was filled with his presence.

She shivered, then said shakily, "We both agreed in Banff that we couldn't just pick up from where we left off, didn't we?"

Lance made no reply; his stare was hard, impassive.

"Well, I was right. It . . ." Haley's voice trailed off, unsure of how to phrase properly what she meant.

"Let me ask you something," Lance said suddenly. "Can you tell me that you were simply faking the pleasure we both shared together while there? Was it all just an act?"

God, no! Haley wanted to cry out. She would never, ever be able to forget that most wonderful, purely blissful episode in her life. But it would serve no purpose to let on to the fact. No, she would do better to allow him to believe that it hadn't meant that

165

much to her. He would never understand her not wanting to continue a one-sided affair. He would certainly never understand that Julia had been right, in her cruel way, in predicting that Haley could never handle a man like Lance. She couldn't. For her sanity she would have to break it off. And it had to be now.

"No," she began her reply softly. "I did have . . . quite a good time while we were there. And I'll always be grateful for having had the opportunity to work in your restaurant. But . . . it simply didn't mean that much. . . . I mean—"

Lance uttered a gruff sound, and Haley flinched as he followed it with a crude expletive. "Save the crap, would you?"

Haley stared at him mutely, shocked at his rancorous tone. He surprised her further by taking the few steps into the living room and sitting down in one corner of the love seat, crossing one ankle over the opposite knee casually. Haley just looked at him, unable to move.

"Julia was here, wasn't she?"

Haley blinked. "How—"

"She called me. Muttering all kinds of garbage as usual. She spoke your name a couple of times, but I was barely paying any attention." He paused and regarded Haley wryly. "What sort of trash did she lay on you this time?"

Haley bit her lower lip and averted her gaze. "It—it wasn't trash, Lance. It was the truth."

"All right, then. Let's hear it."

Haley remained silent, so Lance began speaking.

166

"She told you about how uncaring I am, how cruel, wrapped up only in my business."

Haley glanced boldly at him. "It's true, though, Lance," she said quietly. "Ever since I've known you, you've been wrapped up in your restaurants."

Lance's eyes narrowed a fraction. "And what if I still am? What's so wrong with it?"

Haley felt the muscles in her face twitch spasmodically. It took every ounce of resolve she had not to break down right there.

"I—I'm sorry, Lance. You just confirmed it yourself, don't you see? Why would it be any different with us than it was with you and Julia?" She shook her head. "Please, I—I don't want to see you again. P-please, go."

Lance's eyes narrowed to bare slits, and his jaw hardened visibly. After several painful minutes of dead silence, he rose, snatched up his jacket, and slung it across one shoulder. His footsteps clicked smartly on the tiled entry hall, then stopped as he placed one hand on the doorknob.

"No, I guess you're right. It wouldn't be any different between us. You're just as damn immature and ignorant as your so-called best friend. I only regret I didn't recognize that fact sooner."

Haley had looked over to him as he said that last part, but she quickly glanced away as he pulled roughly on the door. The loud slam of it caused her to jump, shattering the silence as it did her soul into a million shards of agonizing remorse.

CHAPTER ELEVEN

Life, Haley discovered with painful astonishment, did have its way of carrying on. Like a child wary of every new step, she slowly picked up the pieces of her shattered emotions, careful not to deal too intimately with the inner turmoil she kept at precarious bay, lest she collapse from the overwhelming weight of it.

After the first agonizing twenty-fours hours she regained a better hold over herself, going through the motions of normal life with a clarity of purpose that was lifesaving. She had the sense to thank her good fortune for the new job she had recently acquired. Had it not been for that, she felt certain she would not have been able to cope.

Her sleep, however, suffered greatly, diminishing the vitality and strength she usually possessed in abundance. Everything, every small detail of everyday living, seemed to require the greatest of efforts, as if she were functioning with some great weight strapped around her, pulling her backward when she should have been going forward.

Surprisingly, though, she was able to continue with her work according to the schedule she had originally worked out. She did it all within a daze; later she was able to see it as nature's way of providing a much needed protection for her sorely affected psyche.

On Friday evening Mrs. Jordenson telephoned, extending an invitation for Haley to join both her and Mr. Jordenson Saturday night for supper. Haley accepted, recognizing her own need for company. At any other time she would have accepted with a great deal more enthusiasm, but she was at a loss to produce any today. Her mother, of course, immediately questioned Haley's rather reserved mood, but Haley merely attributed it to her increased work load.

Haley was, of course, happy to see her father, and did enjoy several minutes worth of relaxed, mood-dispelling conversation before their supper on Saturday evening. It was not until after the meal, as she helped her mother with cleaning up in the kitchen, that Haley was sharply reminded of the painful situation she had been able to put out of mind for a short while that evening.

"Haley, dear, I'll load the dishwasher if you can clear the table," Mrs. Jordenson suggested in her usual good-humored manner.

"Sure," Haley agreed, finishing the last of a second cup of coffee before walking back into the dining room to begin.

"Have you seen Julia yet, honey?" her mother called out from the kitchen, totally unaware of the sudden trembling her innocent question provoked in Haley's hands.

"Uh . . . yes." Haley spoke slowly, mentally gathering her wits about her. She should have guessed her mother would bring up the subject. Why was she so unprepared for it? But then, everything seemed out of kilter lately.

She walked back into the kitchen, depositing the load of dishes she had gathered from the dining room table onto the Formica counter next to the sink. Mrs.

Jordenson's eyebrows were raised questioningly as she paused while scrubbing a skillet under running water.

"You did? When was that? How was she?"

Her mother was merely expressing innocent curiosity, yet Haley found it extremely difficult to disguise her impatience with the question.

"Actually she came over to visit me," Haley said, returning to the dining room to round up table linen and silverware.

"Oh. Well, that was nice. How is she coming along? Is she much improved?"

"I suppose you could say that," Haley replied, thinking how much she'd rather change the subject.

"Well, I'm glad to hear it. What did you two talk about?"

Haley placed the bundle of soiled napkins and silverware on the counter with a bit more effort than was necessary. Mrs. Jordenson's persistence snapped her patience and she replied in an annoyed tone.

"Really, Mother, it wasn't that interesting. I don't know why you'd even care to know." She moved around to her mother's opposite side, snatching up a dish towel, running it under the faucet, squeezing it out, and turning back toward the dining room. She didn't get far, however, as Mrs. Jordenson suddenly placed a restraining hand on her arm.

"Just a minute, Haley," she said evenly, the level gaze she directed toward her daughter at once demanding and uncompromising. Her eyes narrowed as she added, "You haven't been yourself all night." Upon Haley's attempted objection she silenced her.

"No, just listen to me. It's not just the fact that I'm

170

your mother that enables me to see that you're upset about something. My bringing up Julia seems to be the straw that broke the camel's back. Now . . . don't you think it would help to get it off your chest?"

With Haley's hesitation Mrs. Jordenson coaxed her further, dropping her voice as she continued. "I don't doubt that your father noticed your moodiness tonight also. I won't have him worrying about you, Haley. Whatever is wrong, you're not the type to cover it up. At least not well enough for it to be unnoticeable."

Haley stared balefully at her mother for a long moment, finally lowering her head and letting out a long sigh. She couldn't put up an argument to that. Her mother's intuition would have been enough to tell her that something was troubling her daughter, but Haley had to admit that she probably was wearing her heart on her sleeve, so to speak. And the last thing she wanted to be guilty of was causing her father unnecessary worry. Besides, her mother would have to find out the truth about the situation with Julia at some point. She might as well get it over with now.

"All right," she relented, placing the dish towel on the countertop and slumping back against it.

"Julia and I aren't friends anymore, Mother," she began. "We haven't been for some time now, and we certainly will never be again in the future."

Mrs. Jordenson's head cocked to one side, her eyes widening in surprise at her daughter's statement.

"You can't mean that. Why, Haley, you've known Julia since you were a little girl. You've been friends for such a long time. It seems impossible that—"

"I know. I'm sure this must come as a surprise to you. That's why I didn't want to discuss it."

"But, honey, even the best of friends have conflicts —even terrible arguments. It shouldn't mean the end of the relationship. If that were the case, I'd have lost a lot of friends a long, long time ago."

"Mother," Haley said on a sigh, "you have to believe me. The split between Julia and me is based on much more than a simple disagreement. Or even a terrible argument."

Mrs. Jordenson stared at her daughter in silent expectation of a further explanation. For a brief moment Haley considered omitting the real issue, fabricating some believable story that would satisfy her mother's need to know and her own reluctance to discuss the matter that jabbed so painfully at the very heart of her being. But it wouldn't work, Haley realized. She could never continue to hide what would surely haunt her for the rest of her life. It would be better to get the truth out now than to spend the rest of her days inventing new ways to cover it up.

"Mine and Julia's relationship ended, in reality, before her wedding. It will never be the same for either of us."

Mrs. Jordenson shook her head in bafflement, and Haley continued. "We were in love with the same man." Haley glanced downward and added, "I suppose we still are." Her mother's sharp intake of breath brought her head up quickly, and Haley felt a pang at the obvious anxiety her revelation had suddenly produced.

"I know how crazy and weird this must strike you,

172

Mom," Haley continued in an apologetic tone, "but I had to tell you the truth. It's what you wanted."

"Yes, dear, it is" was her mother's softly spoken reply. Reaching out, she grasped her daughter's hand. "Come on, let's forget about the kitchen for a while. I'd rather hear all this sitting down."

Immensely relieved at her mother's calm, rational acceptance of her story, Haley joined her in the formal living room. Without further prompting, Haley opened up completely, revealing everything about her and Lance's affair before he and Julia were married, all the sordid details of how Julia had cheated him into marrying her, a briefer description of the resumption of their relationship in Banff, and finally, how she had broken it off completely as soon as Lance had telephoned.

Mrs. Jordenson shook her head sadly, sorrow for all the pain her daughter had endured all this time softening her shocked expression, unshed tears glistening brightly in her eyes.

"Honey, I never realized that was your real reason for leaving after graduation. It makes me sick to think you carried all that with you alone. If only—"

"Of course, you didn't know, Mom. Please, don't blame yourself for what I got myself into. And besides, being on my own did me a lot of good."

"But if your father and I had known all this, we certainly never would have concocted that business arrangement with George Sullivan. That was your real reason for not wanting to take the job, wasn't it?"

Haley nodded. "But it doesn't matter. Really, Mom. I suppose it was for the best. I certainly can't hold it against you for wanting to help my career get off to a good start—which it did. And for that I'll always be grateful to both of you." She glanced down at her hands, surprised to see that they were absently playing with the woolen material of her slacks.

"Maybe I needed that one last try with Lance to set it all to rest," she said softly. The words were said, Haley realized even as she spoke them, as much to convince herself as her mother. But whom was she kidding? she wondered later. Certainly not herself. Nothing had been laid to rest as far as her emotional attachment to Lance went. How long did it take to get over something like that? she questioned as she lay in bed that night. Would the pain ever fade away completely, or would it merely become an ordinary thing, a lifetime burden that she would carry forever within her breast? If that was the case, then would she ever know true happiness again? Somehow she thought not.

Confiding in her mother had eased the burden more than she had thought it would, but in spite of helping exorcise the curse of Lance's memory, Haley found it exceedingly difficult to discuss the subject beyond that one evening of baring her soul to her mother.

She preferred to leave it alone, and managed to conduct herself in such a reasonable fashion that her parents were actually pleased to see her getting along so well. In this regard, it was she who was now deserving of an Oscar, for it was all a carefully executed, albeit exceedingly painful act. On the surface she was well on the way to recovery, but inside she grieved more than she thought humanly possible.

174

The void Lance's absence created in her life loomed desolately, an ever-widening chasm that could never, ever be breached.

Work, she thought over and over: thank God for work. She threw herself into it during the next week, surrounding herself in such a quagmire of detail that she barely had time to eat, much less think about anything else. The deprivation the continuous activity was wreaking on her physical being was telling, although she was personally blinded to the fact.

It wasn't until the end of the week, when she had driven to her parents' for her now routine weekly supper with them, that the subject was thrown in her face. Mrs. Jordenson, noticing the drastic change in her daughter's appearance the minute she walked through the door, took her aside immediately for a not-so-gentle mother-to-daughter talk. Once more she prevailed upon Haley's consideration of her father's state of health to at least take some pains to cover up the almost sickly appearance she now made.

Agreeing, Haley visited the bathroom, and after one glance in the mirror, conceded that her mother's admonitions were indeed well founded. She had lost weight, and the normally slight depressions beneath her eyes had deepened into dark half moons. She fumbled among the few cosmetics she had in her purse and repaired her face as best she could. Running a brush through her hair, she fluffed it out and teased it a bit, adding much-needed body that she was nowadays too tired to bother with.

Mrs. Jordenson was placated for the time being, and the three of them enjoyed a relaxing supper.

175

Haley was coaxed into staying later that evening, since, as her father insisted, tomorrow was Saturday. Her mother insisted that her help was not needed in the kitchen, so Haley retired with her father to the den to talk and watch television. By ten o'clock, though, she was growing tired and sleepy, and thought that perhaps she might even fall asleep at a normal hour.

"All right, dear," her mother relented after Haley expressed her desire to call it a night. "I'll get your coat for you."

Haley stood just as the nightly news program was coming on, raising both arms over her head and stretching, indulging in a wide, uninhibited yawn.

"Are you sure you won't fall asleep at the wheel?" Mr. Jordenson asked, standing and moving to switch the television station.

"I'm sure," Haley said, grinning. "What's wrong with Channel Four?"

Her father waved a dismissing hand toward the set. "Bunch of misplaced comedians," he said derisively. "By the time those guys get through spicing up their deliveries with their personal jokes, you wonder what the hell the news was."

Haley laughed at her father's apt appraisal of the seemingly catching trend among the local television news programs. She was about to comment that she agreed wholeheartedly when she stopped, her mouth remaining agape with unspoken words as she stood stock-still, listening in stunned disbelief at what the anchorman was saying.

"Authorities with the Denver Fire Department are not revealing any information concerning the cause of the three-alarm fire that totally devastated one of the six Sullivan restaurants in the Denver metropolis. Arson is suspected, but further evidence is needed to ascertain the actual cause of the fire. The fire occurred late this afternoon, before the restaurant opened its doors to patrons. Several injuries were reported, three of them suffered by firefighters overcome by smoke inhalation. All three have been treated in local hospitals and released. The owner of the popular restaurant chain, Lance Sullivan, however, is reported to have been visiting the restaurant at time of the fire breakout, and did sustain injuries. Hospital spokespersons, however, are not offering any comments as to the extent of those injuries at the present time."

The newscaster's voice went on to his next story, and Haley could vaguely hear her father's voice commenting on the shocking report. She stood transfixed, her physical sensations reduced to a single awareness of the sound of her heart's furiously pounding beat. It was too incredible, too impossible, she thought wildly. Not Lance—oh, please, God, not Lance!

Unaware of the ashen appearance her skin had taken on, Haley barely heard her father calling out to her mother, nor felt both their hands on her shoulders and arms, guiding her toward the couch, gently pushing her back down onto it.

Something cold and wet was on her forehead, and only when Haley made a sound of objection, reaching up instinctively to push it away, did she realize that she was lying down on the couch, her mother sitting beside her as she held a damp cloth to Haley's forehead.

"Wha—" Haley mumbled, trying to push herself up on her elbows.

"Just lie back down for a moment," Mrs. Jordenson said, gently pushing her back down. "You almost passed out."

"Lance . . . Lance is . . ." Haley's voice trailed away on a sob.

"Your father is on the telephone right now. He called George, but he wasn't there. The family is at the hospital. He's trying to get a message through to them now."

"I have to see him," Haley said, her voice more forceful as she regained her strength. Insistently she shoved her mother's hand away and sat up, rubbing her face and running both hands through her hair. She could hear her father speaking on the telephone in the kitchen, hanging up shortly, and walking back in to the den.

He stood in the doorway, hands on his hips, concern etched across his features. "I couldn't get through to anyone in the family, and the personnel at the hospital weren't much help. All I could do was leave a message."

"I have to go," Haley said, making an effort to stand. Her mother's hand restrained her.

"Honey, wait. You're still in shock. I don't think—"

"I'm going to the hospital," Haley said, shrugging out of her mother's grasp. She glanced from one parent to the other. "I have to see him." Determinedly she stood up.

Mr. Jordenson pursed his lips together and cast a meaningful glance at his wife. "Why don't you drive her there, Rita? I'll stay in case someone returns the call."

Mrs. Jordenson nodded. "Let me get my coat and the keys." She walked quickly from the room, and Haley blindly slipped into her own coat. Her mother was back shortly and after bidding Mr. Jordenson good night, they left the house through the back door, the frigid night air shocking Haley into sharp awareness.

The ride to the hospital was agonizing. Haley was grateful that her mother was driving, not at all sure how she could have handled the situation alone. Later Haley was to wonder how she made it through that long, anguishing ride, wondering if Lance was alive or dead. She was amazed at the inner strength she found to get her through the long, shattering night.

She barely remembered being led through a maze of hospital corridors, greeting the Sullivan family, waiting until she was given permission to see Lance. Her initial relief that he was alive gradually subsided to a worry at what she and the others would discover when they were finally allowed to see him.

The physician handling the case finally appeared, his report bringing tears of joy to all present. Lance had suffered very minor burns on one hand and had been overcome by smoke inhalation. He was going to be all right, although he would need to stay in the hopital for an additional forty-eight hours.

As the others sat and spoke in quiet, though noticeably lighter tones, Haley moved to stand alone beside the window of the small waiting area, hands crossed over her chest, gazing out into the starry blackness of the sky. Gradually, without warning, bits and pieces of her conversation with Julia that terrible day in her town house filtered into her consciousness, gaining hold of her attention until she was filled with an awesome consideration. As Julia's words came back to her Haley was suddenly struck by the realization that she had taken only what she had wanted to hear from the conversation, ignoring whatever could have possibly prevented all this from happening.

How was it Julia had put it? Something to the effect that it would take something drastic for Lance to get his mind on anything other than his business. God, what had she been saying? Haley wondered, her stomach turning at the possibility of it. Could Julia have instigated something so terrible, so drastic as what had happened today to prove her point? Haley shuddered at the import of that thought. If it were so—and Lord help the woman if it was the case—then Haley was to blame in this tragedy.

With a flood of soul-searing guilt Haley realized that by not telling Lance of Julia's visit, by not telling him everything the woman had said and implied, she had possibly endangered his life. Why hadn't she told him? Why had she clung to her pride and pretended

180

that she no longer cared to continue their relationship—an outright lie?

"Miss Jordenson, you can go in now." Haley turned and sought out the voice that beckoned to her. A nurse was standing in the doorway of the waiting area, and as the others watched quietly Haley followed her down the hall toward Lance's room.

It was immediately obvious he hadn't been expecting her; the surprise on his face revealed it all too clearly. Haley's breathing was coming now in rapid, shallow spurts, the mere sight of him like some sparkling oasis in the middle of a burning desert.

The pale green eyes that watched her as she approached were warily appraising, as if suspicious of her motives for being here. But Haley didn't care; she was filled with an intense happiness that the man lying before her was the same Lance she remembered, his virile potency overriding any telltale signs of physical weakness he might have been suffering at the moment. His day's growth of beard and the tousled golden brown locks against the pillow were all the more enhancing to his ruggedness.

"Hello, Haley." Lance spoke first, the pale green eyes casually taking in her appearance. "You've lost weight." It was a flat, clinical statement, one that Haley found amusing, considering that it was he, not she, who was the patient.

"A little," she said, moving instinctively closer to the bed, her thighs resting against the metal frame.

"Why did you come?" The bluntness of the question startled her, and for a moment she was stymied as to an answer.

181

Spasmodically she swallowed. "I heard . . . that you were injured. On television. No one would tell us how you were."

Lance raised one eyebrow speculatively. "And you had to come and see for yourself?"

Haley nodded mutely.

"But why?" he persisted.

How could he be so suspicious of her motives, Haley wondered painfully. "I wanted to make sure that you were all right," she answered defensively.

"And I could ask why to that, couldn't I?"

Her frustration at his boorishness began to take its toll, and she swallowed again, this time in an effort to dispel the ever-expanding lump in her throat. Tears were smarting in her eyes now, and she turned abruptly to wipe them away with the back of her hand.

Another hand, large and determined, grasped her upper arm, clamping tightly about it until she turned back to face him. She stared at him wide-eyed, her features threatening to crumple momentarily as she struggled to hold back the dam of her emotions.

"I'd like an answer, Haley," Lance insisted, the pale green irises hardening, clearly indicating there would be no further sidestepping on her part.

"I came—" Haley began in a scratchy voice, amber orbs lowered to study the hair-roughened hand still planted firmly around her arm. She cleared her throat and spoke again, this time jumping in head first. "I came because I love you."

There was silence, and Haley dared not raise her eyes for fear of the disdain that surely would mar

Lance's features now. She waited in breathless fear, half expecting him to order her from the room.

"Why didn't you ever tell me?" Lance asked quietly, his hold on her arm loosening now as his hand slipped down to hold hers within it.

"I—I didn't think it would matter to you. I knew you didn't love me, and I—I thought it best not to burden you with my feelings."

Lance gave a gruff laugh, and Haley glanced up at him.

"*Burden* me! Is that why you said you didn't want to see me anymore? Because you didn't want to burden me with your love?"

Haley chewed her lower lip to stop its sudden quivering. Any moment now and the dam would break. . . .

"You astound me, you know that? For such an nice person, you're unbelievably arrogant. You assume so much for other people. What gives you the right to decide what is and what isn't a burden for other people?"

Haley stared at Lance in disbelief. This wasn't exactly the response she had thought was forthcoming. Disapproval, rejection—yes. But certainly not a lecture on her personality.

Lance shook his head and crossed his arms over his chest, his gray-green gaze regarding her skeptically. "What about my supposed workaholism? Doesn't that still bother you?"

Absently Haley fingered the edge of the sheet covering him. "Don't make fun of me, Lance," she said softly.

"Is that what you think I'm doing? Well, I'm not.

183

I don't want to hear any of this unless you mean it. Unless you've come to terms with the doubts you have about me."

Haley said nothing, and after a few moments of silence she felt his strong, square fingertips on her chin. Slowly she lifted her gaze to meet his.

"I could never treat you the same as Julia," he stated. "The differences between the two of you are as drastic as night and day." Slowly his eyes traveled across her face, soaking in every detail of her expression, then stopped once more to meet her amber gaze.

"Tell me something. Did you think just because I never told you I loved you, that I didn't? Did you ever tell me before tonight that you loved me?"

Haley felt her heart leap with the words she was hearing. Was he saying he loved her? Her head moved slowly from side to side as she stared at him in bewilderment.

"No. I don't guess I ever did," she answered.

"So." Lance shrugged a shoulder, his eyes narrowing slightly. "The words don't really mean that much, do they? We've both loved each other all along, and neither of us found the words necessary." Haley's eyes were shimmering now from tears of a different nature: wondrous joy that she was hearing the very vow she had come to believe would never, ever be said.

"Oh, Lance, if I had known . . ."

"What would you have done had you known?" Lance asked, his expression softening as he tugged on her arm, pulling her down to sit on the edge of the bed.

"Oh. So much. So very much," Haley whispered, bending forward to press her lips lightly against his tawny brow.

"Tell me about it," Lance said in a low voice, curling one hand behind her nape as she rested her head on his chest.

And she did. She told him everything that had happened concerning Julia's visit. He expressed no surprise at anything Julia had implied, but Haley's suspicion that Julia may have had a hand in the fire was laid to rest when Lance revealed that the cause had been pinned down to an electrical problem that had not been taken care of. Julia, he assured her, could not have had anything to do with the fire. She had called a week earlier, shortly after her visit with Haley, informing him that she had found a job and was moving to California to live with one of her old college chums.

The news of it was almost overwhelming, and Haley found herself smiling—a genuine ear-to-ear smile that nourished her very soul.

"Not bad," Lance commented, lifting her to study the look of mirth on her tear-stained cheeks.

"What do you mean?" Haley asked, sniffing.

"When you smile, it makes you look fatter."

Haley clicked her tongue and narrowed her eyes. "Now, why should you want me to look fatter?"

"Because," Lance said throatily, pulling her back down to him, his lips grazing the edge of her jaw, his warm breath filling her with a need that made her tingle all over, "I want"—his lips covered hers, tasting their round fullness—"my wife"—her lips parted, accepting the velvet roughness of his—"to be fat and sassy."

Haley's giggle was a short-lived sound, gradually fading into a sweet beckoning groan that Lance was only too willing to appease.

LOOK FOR NEXT MONTH'S
CANDLELIGHT ECSTASY ROMANCES ®

Seize The Dawn
by Vanessa Royall

For as long as she could remember, Elizabeth Rolfson knew that her destiny lay in America. She arrived in Chicago in 1885, the stunning heiress to a vast empire. As men of daring pressed westward, vying for the land, Elizabeth was swept into the savage struggle. Driven to learn the secret of her past, to find the one man who could still the restlessness of her heart, she would stand alone against the mighty to claim her proud birthright and grasp a dream of undying love.

A DELL BOOK   17788-X $3.50

A woman's place—the parlor, not the concert stage! But radiant Diana Ballantyne, pianist extraordinaire, had one year before she would bow to her father's wishes, return to England and marry. She had given her word, yet the moment she met the brilliant Maestro, Baron Lukas von Korda, her fate was sealed. He touched her soul with music, kissed her lips with fire, filled her with unnameable desire. One minute warm and passionate, the next aloof, he mystified her, tantalized her. She longed for artistic triumph, ached for surrender, her passions ignited by Vienna dreams.

A DELL BOOK   19530-6 $3.50

Vienna Dreams

by JANETTE RADCLIFFE